P9-CMX-421

He walked her to the elevator. All the while, she wasn't sure what to make of him. Was he really going to consider her offer? Or was he just stringing her along?

When the elevator door slid open, she turned to him. "Thank you for dinner. And the view. I loved the view."

He surprised her with a smile. It lit up his eyes and made him look younger and sexier, if that was possible. His gaze lowered to her lips. "It is a spectacular view."

And suddenly she had the distinct impression they weren't talking about the same thing. Her heart pitter-pattered faster as she grew warm. They definitely weren't talking about the same thing at all.

If she didn't step on that elevator right this moment, she had the feeling things would spin completely out of control. And she'd done so well negotiating with him. She refused to falter now for, what? A moment of desire? A quick flirtation?

"Good night," she stammered as she forced her feet to move.

"I'll be seeing you soon."

Dear Reader,

Life isn't always sunshine and rainbows, though wouldn't it be nice it if was? Sometimes what you cherish most is threatened. That's the case for Alina Martin as she fights to save her home as well as the patchwork family she's created for herself.

Graham Toliver is also fighting for what's important to him—his father's legacy. Though the family company is in chaos, he's striving to fix it. And this is how the hero and heroine's snowy worlds collide. Because Graham has bought Alina's apartment building, intending to demolish it. Talk about a lousy Christmas present.

But Alina refuses to give up. She plans to show Graham the specialness of Stirling Apartments. And with some holiday magic, they begin to see each other as much more than the opposition. In fact, beneath the twinkle of Christmas lights, they find themselves falling for each other. But will it be enough to see them through their challenges?

Because when all is said and done, one person may have to give up what they desire most. And it may not be what they started out wanting—a home or a legacy—it might be something much dearer.

Happy reading,

Jennifer

Fairytale Christmas with the Millionaire

Jennifer Faye

If you purchased this book without a cover you should be aware that this book is stolen property. It was reported as "unsold and destroyed" to the publisher, and neither the author nor the publisher has received any payment for this "stripped book."

Recycling programs for this product may not exist in your area.

ISBN-13: 978-1-335-55657-8

Fairytale Christmas with the Millionaire

Copyright © 2020 by Jennifer F. Stroka

All rights reserved. No part of this book may be used or reproduced in any manner whatsoever without written permission except in the case of brief quotations embodied in critical articles and reviews.

This is a work of fiction. Names, characters, places and incidents are either the product of the author's imagination or are used fictitiously. Any resemblance to actual persons, living or dead, businesses, companies, events or locales is entirely coincidental.

This edition published by arrangement with Harlequin Books S.A.

For questions and comments about the quality of this book, please contact us at CustomerService@Harlequin.com.

Harlequin Enterprises ULC
22 Adelaide St. West, 40th Floor
Toronto, Ontario M5H 4E3, Canada
www.Harlequin.com

Printed in U.S.A.

Award-winning author **Jennifer Faye** pens fun,
heartwarming contemporary romances with rugged
cowboys, sexy billionaires and enchanting royalty.
Internationally published, with books translated
into nine languages, she is a two-time winner of the
RT Book Reviews Reviewers' Choice Award. She
has also won the CataRomance Reviewers' Choice
Award, been named a Top Pick author and been
nominated for numerous other awards.

Books by Jennifer Faye

Harlequin Romance

The Bartolini Legacy

The Prince and the Wedding Planner
The CEO, the Puppy and Me
The Italian's Unexpected Heir

Greek Island Brides

Carrying the Greek Tycoon's Baby
Claiming the Drakos Heir
Wearing the Greek Millionaire's Ring

The Cattaneos' Christmas Miracles

Heiress's Royal Baby Bombshell

Once Upon a Fairytale

Beauty and Her Boss
Miss White and the Seventh Heir

Snowbound with an Heiress
Her Christmas Pregnancy Surprise

Visit the Author Profile page
at Harlequin.com for more titles.

Praise for
Jennifer Faye

"This talented author once again excels in her talent as a storyteller. Grabbing your attention from the first page to the last, the story is touching and at times heartbreaking. Another beautiful story that will stay with you for a very long time."

—*Goodreads* on *Her Christmas Pregnancy Surprise*

CHAPTER ONE

CHRISTMAS WAS IN the air...

Cheerful holiday tunes played on the radio. The Manhattan storefronts were trimmed in shiny tinsel and twinkle lights. And right here on Holly Lane, the Stirling Apartments' foyer was decked out with lush garland and a pencil Christmas tree adorned with white lights and red satin balls.

This was hands down Alina Martin's favorite time of the year. She loved to sing the uplifting carols, all the while pretending she could carry a tune. She loved to decorate the tree. And she loved how the holiday season brought out the best in people. However, this year she was hoping for a Christmas miracle to keep her from losing her beloved home.

But at the moment, her immediate attention was focused on finding her apron. Mentally she recounted her actions the prior evening. The day hadn't been much out of the ordinary. She'd worked the morning shift at the restaurant tending to the party planning as well as helping out in the dining room before rushing home to do her second job as building manager. Even with a rent-controlled apartment, it wasn't cheap living in New York City. And yet there was nowhere else in the world she'd rather live.

"Mrrrr..."

She glanced down to find her ginger cat, who she'd affectionately named Prince. They'd first met at a local park. She'd been out for a walk, trying to achieve her ten thousand steps a day, when she'd stopped at a local animal rescue adopt-a-thon. Long story short, Prince picked her out and the rest was history.

When Prince rubbed against her leg, she said, "Begging won't work. You already had breakfast."

"Meow."

Sometimes it was like he could truly understand what she said, "Sorry, sweetie, I can't hold you, either. I have to leave."

"Mrrrr..."

He strode away, probably headed back to bed. She wished she could join him.

Alina turned her focus back to her missing apron. She rushed over to the dryer, where she found it at the back of the machine. It was a bit wrinkled. She shook it out with a couple of quick snaps. Good enough.

She rolled up her apron and then stuffed it in her oversize purse. She threw on her red winter coat, a knit cap and her boots. Out the door she went. Noticing the elevator was at the top floor, she opted for the stairs instead. Hers wasn't a large building, not by New York City standards. But within its five floors, it housed the people she liked to refer to as her adopted family.

She exited the stairwell and rushed up the hallway. Meg, her best friend, stood in the lobby near the mailboxes. Her curly red hair was pulled back in a ponytail. However, instead of her usual sunny smile, she wore a distinct frown. Meg held up a letter. "Have you seen this?"

The worry in her friend's warm brown eyes drew Alina's concern. "What is it?"

"It's another letter about them throwing us out."

"What?" Alina rushed over to her mailbox. In her rush, she fumbled with her keys. They fell to the tile floor with a loud jangle.

With a groan of frustration, she bent over to retrieve the keys. Once the little door was open, she withdrew her copy of the letter. Her gaze scanned down over it. The new owner was willing to pay them extra to move out by the new year. That wasn't going to happen.

With her back to the front door, Alina faced her friend. "Don't worry. There's nothing Toliver can do to rush things. He has to wait ninety days before he can begin eviction proceedings."

"But that's in February. Even that's not much time to find a new place to live."

One of their youngest and newest residents, Jimmy Greene, came rushing past them. He gave a quick nod in greeting but kept going. He must have another interview lined up at a software company. He'd inherited his grandmother's rent-controlled apartment and was now struggling to find a job in the competitive market of online video gaming.

The door creaked open and closed behind him, letting the cold winter air rush in around them. It also reminded Alina that she had to get a move on.

"We'll figure something out," Alina said, hoping her voice sounded encouraging. "Even if I have to go back to that awful man's office building and stage another protest in the foyer until he agrees to meet with me. From what I've read, he inherited his position and he doesn't know what he's doing. Well, that's obvious." She held up her copy of the letter as proof. "This isn't going to change Stirling residents' minds about moving. I've got to get to work. We'll talk later."

"I've got to get going, too. Remember, I have that weeklong seminar in LA. And then I'm spending the next couple of weeks in Wyoming with my parents. But I can cancel—the family visit, not the seminar—if you need me."

"No. Go. Enjoy yourself. You haven't seen your family in a year. I've got this."

Uncertainty showed in Meg's eyes. "You're sure?"

"Positive."

"Keep me updated."

"I will." Alina gave her a brief hug. "We'll talk soon."

Alina spun around and immediately bumped into a solid force. She lifted her gaze, finding a tall man standing there. It was his brown eyes that immediately caught her attention. They were dark and mysterious. And she found herself drawn in by them.

The more she stared, the more she noticed a glint of irritation. Well, it wasn't her fault he was standing in the middle of the foyer.

"Sorry," she mumbled. And then she rushed right past him.

She'd have to run if she was to catch her train. She set off as quickly as she dared in the wet snow. As she kept moving, her thoughts returned to the mystery man in the lobby. Who was he? And what was he doing in her building? Well, it wasn't her building but it was starting to feel that way because not only was she the building manager but she had also been unofficially elected to lead the charge to save the Stirling from being torn down and replaced by a flashy high-rise.

Though she didn't relish the idea, perhaps it was time she made another visit to Mr. Toliver's office. She'd been turned away before for not having an appointment. The problem was that every time she'd tried to set up an appointment, he was either away on business or unavailable for the foreseeable future. She was pretty certain they'd been delay tactics and he'd been in his office the whole time.

And when she'd staged a peaceful protest with other Stirling residents, hoping Mr. Toliver would no longer be able to ignore them, the police had been called. Her blood boiled every time she thought of that man avoiding her—avoiding the truth about the damage he was doing to people's lives. The next time she wouldn't be chased away so easily.

His teeth ground together.

Graham Toliver couldn't believe those two young women had been bad-mouthing him— right in front of him no less. Surely they'd heard the outside door open when that young man held the door for him to enter.

Still, those women had kept talking, and not quietly, either. Hadn't they heard his approaching footsteps? It wasn't like he tiptoed around. Or hadn't they cared who overheard them?

His muscles tensed. It was bad enough not having the confidence of his board but to have perfect strangers judge his qualifications to run his family's business, well, that was quite another thing.

He was tempted to withdraw his very generous offer to get them to move out earlier. But he hesitated. He was a businessman above all else. He drew in a deep breath and then slowly blew it out.

He recalled the young woman with light blond hair and pink stripes streaked through it. When she'd bumped into him, their gazes had connected. For just a moment, it felt as though time had stood still. It was though he should know her, but he was positive they'd never met. He wouldn't have forgotten those blue eyes framed by long, dark lashes.

No matter how cute he might find her, he couldn't dismiss her words. Still, he shouldn't let that rude woman's words get to him. It was quite likely they'd never see each other again.

Instead of thinking of her mesmerizing eyes and how they'd made his heart jolt, he needed to focus on the reason for his visit. He was here to speak with the building manager. He withdrew a slip of paper from his pocket with a hastily scrawled name...

Did that say Al? He squinted. It didn't help sort the squiggly line into letters. Now he was left to guess at the name. Alan? It seemed like a safe bet. As for the last name, it was easier to read. Martin. Alan Martin? Perhaps.

When he glanced up, he found he was alone in the lobby. He wasn't used to people just strolling right by him like he was a nobody. At the office, people always wanted something from him. A signature here, an answer to a question there. It was always something. But at the Stirling Apartments, no one recognized him. Interesting.

For a moment, he wondered what it'd be like to not be the CEO of a billion-dollar business. A frown pulled at the corners of his mouth. That would never happen. Toliver Investments was his destiny. Without it, he'd be—well, he'd be nothing.

He made his way farther into the building. This Al or Alan guy shouldn't be too hard to find as he was the building manager. And just like that, Graham happened upon a door with a black plaque that read Building Manager.

Graham rapped his knuckles on the door. No response. He checked the time. It wasn't quite eight o'clock. Surely the guy would be at work by now. Didn't everyone arrive early? His employees did.

Just as he raised his hand to knock once more, a door farther down the hall opened. An older man stepped into the hallway. They nodded to each other, then Graham turned his attention back to the door and knocked louder this time. Again, no sounds came from inside.

When the older man ambled down the hallway, Graham cleared his throat. "Excuse me. Do you know where I can find…" He glanced at the slip of paper once more. "An Al or Alan Martin?"

A smile lifted beneath the man's bushy white mustache. "Try the Christmas Café."

Why would he try there? But before he could formulate the question, the man had disappeared onto the nearby elevator. Graham glanced around for someone else to ask but the hallway was empty.

It would have helped if his investigator had left him a phone number for the building manager. After all, he had to find this Al guy. He was obviously getting the tenants worked up about not moving—as was evidenced by the two young women Graham had encountered in the lobby.

He once more glanced at his Rolex. Time was ticking by and he'd missed breakfast this morning. He supposed a quick stop at the Christmas Café wouldn't be so bad. He'd promised his board he'd make progress on getting the tenants to move out early—by the beginning of the year—

because time was money and money spoke volumes at board meetings.

And so he set off for the restaurant. Once he tracked down this Alan guy, Graham was determined they'd come to some sort of resolution. He just had to find out the guy's price.

CHAPTER TWO

SHE'D MADE IT to work with literally a minute to spare.

Alina didn't like to be late for anything. Her father used to say it was a trait she'd inherited from her mother. Alina had to take his word for it because she'd been too young when her mother had passed for her to remember those sorts of details.

What she did remember of her mother was that she was kind and loving. She remembered her mother's smile; it was bright and glowing, warm and welcoming. But sometimes Alina wondered if that was a real memory or just something she'd picked up from staring at her mother's pictures—the ones she'd been able to salvage and hide from her wicked stepmother. Once Alina's father had remarried, her stepmother had rid their Manhattan apartment of everything that was a remembrance of Alina's mother—as though she could just wipe away the past.

But when it came to Alina, her stepmother couldn't just toss her out with the trash. Though

Alina knew if she could, her stepmother would have done exactly that. Alina's father used to say Alina was the spitting image of her mother. Alina didn't see it. Not really. But everyone who had known her mother agreed. She was her mother's mini-me.

Alina pushed aside thoughts of the past because if she didn't start taking orders and serving up food, she wouldn't get tipped. And if she didn't get tipped, she wouldn't make her rent payment. And that would just be one more excuse for the new building owner to kick her to the curb as soon as possible.

Alina's mouth pulled into a distinct frown. How could someone be so cold and calculating, especially at this time of the year? Her gaze lifted, taking in the twinkle lights trimming the edge of the ceiling. This upscale restaurant went overboard with the decorations. It was part of its charm. The white walls were now adorned with Christmas prints. Large, red poinsettias were strategically placed about the dining room. A pencil tree stood near the hostess station with white lights and silver ornaments. And then there was Santa all done up in his red velvet and snowy white trim. Next to him were elves in their red overalls and pointed hats.

"Hurry up." Her manager, Sally, softened the order with a smile. "It's going to be a busy day."

"How can you tell?" Alina asked.

"When you've been working here as long as I have, you can feel it in your bones."

Alina arched a brow at Sally. She didn't believe her. There was more to the woman's reliable fortune-telling than feeling it in her bones. The woman definitely had a sixth sense about her.

Sally leaned in and said conspiratorially, "There are going to be flurries all day. No accumulation but enough to put people in the holiday spirit. They'll be out and about trying to put a dent in their Christmas shopping. Mark my words."

"I believe you." And with that Alina tied her apron, not having time to worry about the wrinkles.

The restaurant wasn't overly busy. The early breakfast crowd had moved on. But with this being the holiday season, shoppers would stop by the café off and on all day, in between finding just the right gift for that special someone in their life.

Not that Alina would know about that as her last boyfriend had broken up with her after just six months together. When the former building manager quit and moved to Florida where the winters were so much warmer, she'd taken on the building manager position to help pay off her credit card bills. But having two jobs took up a lot of time. These days she never had time in her busy schedule to go out on dates. She couldn't blame her ex for breaking up with her. When she wasn't working at the restaurant, she was on call to help the Stirling residents with all of their problems. Some she could help with, others she had to call in professionals.

Alina had just turned in an order when Sally walked up to her. "I have someone at one of my tables requesting you. At least I think it's you he wants."

Alina's brows drew together as she smiled at her friend. "You think?"

Sally shrugged. "Thought you'd want to check him out since he's awfully cute and he isn't wearing a ring."

"Let me guess. If you didn't have your own cute husband waiting for you at home, you would have kept him to yourself?"

Sally's smile widened. "How'd you guess?"

Alina shook her head. "I don't need you setting me up. I'm fine on my own. I promise."

"I'm not setting you up." Sally's expression was perfectly serious. "This guy was asking for Alan Martin. He said he was told he could find you here."

"Alan? Seriously?" A lot of people messed up her name but this was really bad. She sighed. "Okay. I'll see what he wants."

Sally pointed her in the direction of a table near the front of the restaurant. Alina wondered what this man wanted. She hoped it wasn't some sort of problem. She didn't need any more problems. She was up to her chin in them.

Her steps were quick. Her orders would be up in a few minutes. And she wasn't going to serve up food that had dried out under the warmer. She wouldn't want to eat food that had been sitting too long and she wouldn't do that to someone else.

With "I'll Be Home for Christmas" playing in the background, Alina approached the table by the big windows overlooking the busy sidewalk. The man had his head down as he read the menu. It gave her a moment to study him. His hair was dark and cut short. Every strand appeared to be in place. He wore a dark suit. It looked expensive.

"Excuse me," she said. "You asked for me."

When he lifted his head, his gaze met hers. Her heart jolted in recognition. She would know those brown eyes anywhere. They were the same ones she'd stared into that very morning in the lobby of her building.

His dark brows drew together as unspoken questions flashed in his eyes. Apparently, she wasn't the only one to remember their run-in. But why had he followed her here? Was he some sort of stalker? Worry sent her pulse racing.

"You. You're the woman from the building this morning." He set aside the menu.

"And you're the man who stood there eavesdropping."

"I did not. I was politely waiting to ask a question."

"If you say so. Still, you could have cleared your throat or said something." The man's gaze grew darker. Good. Let him be angry. She didn't like to be spied upon and she didn't have time to waste. "I have to get back to work."

"But where is Alan?"

"It's Alina. And I'm standing right here, but not for much longer." Her brain said to turn around and walk away, but her feet refused to move.

"Wait." Confusion showed in his eyes. "That can't be right." He reached in his pocket and withdrew a slip of paper. "I'm looking for Al or Alan Martin. He's the building manager at the Stirling Apartments on Holly Lane."

"I'm the building manager."

The man stared at her for a moment as though trying to figure out if he believed her or not. "Can I ask you a question?"

She shrugged. "You can but it doesn't mean I'll answer."

A smile lit up his face, making him downright gorgeous. The breath hitched in her lungs. For a second, she forgot she'd been irritated with him.

She took a moment to really notice him. He was wearing a charcoal gray suit with a brilliant blue dress shirt sans the tie. The top button was undone, revealing a silver chain around his neck. Interesting. Perhaps it wouldn't hurt to give him another chance.

Her gaze rose, taking in a squared jaw that was clean-shaven, until finally she met his dark gaze. She could sense he was quite observant, and right now, he was studying her. What was he seeing in her? And why was he interested in her?

Was he planning to ask her out? A bubble of laughter rose up in her throat. She swallowed hard. This man could easily grace the glossy pages of any magazine—then again, perhaps he already did. Either way, there was no way he'd be interested in plain old her—the memory of her stepmother's insults still lingered in the back of her mind.

"What is the deal with this place?" he asked.

She wasn't sure she understood. "Excuse me?"

"The restaurant, is it really called the Christmas Café?"

"Yes."

His eyes widened. "You mean all year-round?"

She nodded and smiled. "In here, it's Christmas year-round."

"Even in the summer, it's decorated for Christmas?"

"Well, Santa and his buddies do like to celebrate other holidays so they put up valentines, shamrocks, jack o'lanterns, and in the summer, Santa breaks out his board shorts and surfboard."

If it was possible, the man's eyes widened even further. "Seriously?" When she nodded again, he said, "That's a lot of Christmas."

"I take it you're not a fan of the holiday."

"No." There was no hesitation in his very firm answer.

What in the world had made him so grinchy? But she stopped herself from asking. She didn't have time to get to know this man, no matter how cute she might find him or how curious she was to know the man behind those dark, mysterious eyes.

"I really need to get back to work," she said. "Do you want to order?"

"In a moment, but first I need to speak with you about the apartment building."

"Listen, if you're looking for an apartment to rent, you've come to the wrong place."

"Why's that?" His brown eyes sparked with interest.

"Because some company is trying to force out all of the tenants."

"Trying to?"

She shrugged. "They've sent notices but the fight isn't over. In fact, it's just beginning."

"What does that mean?"

Her gaze narrowed in on him. "Why all of the questions? Are you a reporter or something?"

At first, the thought alarmed her. But as she rolled it around in her mind, she warmed up to the possibilities. In fact, the idea of relaying her story to the press became downright appealing. Why hadn't she thought of it a long time ago?

"I'm not a reporter."

"You're not?" Disappointment assailed her. She made a mental note to contact a reporter. "Then what's with all of the questions about the apartment building?"

"I'm the new owner."

What? Surely she hadn't heard him correctly. Her gaze searched his. He seemed to be taking a sort of satisfaction in being able to catch her off guard. It wouldn't happen again.

Was it really that surprising?

Graham watched as Alina gaped at him. He hadn't intended to spring a surprise attack. In fact, he'd been expecting her to recognize him. Perhaps he'd done too good of a job ducking the press since taking over as CEO. The truth was that he'd never wanted to live a public life, not like his father, who made the news regularly.

His father had thought the more press coverage he received, the greater the confirmation of his success—his company's success. And Graham's mother, well, she would have gone along with most anything that would make his father happy. And his father had only been happy when his company was on top of the business world, when his son was on top of his class, when their family's name was on top of the headlines. Second place wasn't good enough.

"You can't be Graham Toliver," she said. "He's much older. I know. I've seen the pictures."

"That was my father, Graham Toliver II. I'm Graham Toliver III." As the light of dawning settled upon her, he hoped they could get down to business. "Could you sit down so we can talk?"

She shook her head. "I'm working."

"This shouldn't take long. I'd like to make you an offer."

She opened her mouth, presumably to refuse to speak with him. But then she pressed her lips together as though rolling the thought around in her mind before deciding. "I'm listening."

"Alina." A server rushed up to them, interrupting before Graham could respond. Her name tag said her name was Sally. "Are you available on Thursday? We just received a big reservation and we could use more help."

"I… I can't. I have work at the building to do."

"Please, Alina," Sally said. "You know how

much these big groups tip. It'll really help you if that jerk kicks you out of your home."

Color rushed to Alina's cheeks. She didn't say anything for the moment. "Let me think about it. Can I let you know?"

"I'll mark you down. If it doesn't work out, you can let me know tomorrow."

This was the first time Graham had a chance to visualize the Stirling residents as flesh and blood and not merely as numbers on a spread-sheet. He thought she'd at least be appreciative of the extra money he was offering—money his company didn't have to hand out.

Alina acted as though he was kicking them to the curb with nothing but their belongings. He'd made them a fair offer to move. And then he'd upped that offer if they moved sooner. In fact, his board had balked at the size of the offer but that hadn't stopped him from making it happen.

Alina turned back to him. "I have to get back to work."

"I tracked you down so we could come to some sort of agreement."

She shook her head. "You wasted your time."

"I can wait, you know, until you have another break." He had meetings all morning but they could be moved. This was more important.

"I won't have a break for hours. I just started

my shift. And I can't just have you sitting here all day taking up space."

"Then have dinner with me." The words were out before he realized how they might sound.

Her eyes widened with surprise. "No."

Ouch! His ego took a direct hit. He wasn't used to being turned down by women. Not that he wanted to date Alina—or anyone else for that matter. He had enough issues to deal with at the office without having to figure out a relationship—something he was not good at, just ask his ex-girlfriend.

"Wait. I didn't mean that as in an actual *date* date." He noticed the color bloom in her cheeks and he couldn't help but think how beautiful she looked. As soon as the thought came to him, he dismissed it. He refused to get distracted. "What I meant was that we could have a business dinner."

She shook her head. "I don't think it's a good idea."

He wasn't going to let this go, even if it meant opening himself up to some pushback. "I thought you wanted to speak to the man who bought your building."

"I do," she said quickly.

"Good." He smiled satisfactorily. "I'll send a car to pick you up at six." He got to his feet.

"What? No."

"Are you saying you aren't interested in pitching your reasons for keeping the building as is?"

"I…uh…sure, I want to."

"Then this is your chance."

She hesitated. "Fine."

They exchanged phone numbers before he left.

The truth was that he didn't want to spend his time listening to all of her sentimental reasons why the building shouldn't be demolished for a new high-rise to be put in its place. He'd never conducted one of these meetings himself, but he'd witnessed his father conduct them.

His father had never been one for patience. He'd barely let the other party get a sentence or two out of their mouth before he'd shut them down. But Graham wasn't his father. And sometimes people just needed to feel as though they'd been heard. He would keep his word and hear Alina out. That didn't mean he would change his mind.

CHAPTER THREE

WHY IN THE world had she agreed?

For the remainder of the day, Alina could think of nothing else but her upcoming date… er, business meeting with Graham. So much so that she'd messed up two orders and received a gentle reprimand from her supervisor. Then upon her return home, she learned Grace Taylor's kitchen sink had a leak. When Alina went to work on it, she'd been distracted by thoughts of what to wear to dinner that evening. When instead of tightening the joint, she'd loosened it and ended up with water in her face. It'd startled her back to reality and she focused on the task at hand.

Once finished with the sink she rushed back to her apartment. Having no idea what to wear to a trendy downtown restaurant, Alina texted her friend Meg. Her friend promptly showed up at her door. "I can't believe you're having dinner with him."

"It's not dinner." When Meg arched a disbelieving brow, Alina said, "Well, it is dinner but it's not like you're thinking. It's all about business. That's it."

"Uh-huh." Meg's tone said she didn't believe her protests.

"It is." Alina ignored the way her heart raced and her heart pounded when she thought about sitting across the table from Graham and staring into his dark mesmerizing eyes as they talked. The enemy shouldn't be so handsome. "Now what should I wear?" She held up a dark pair of jeans with a red cable-knit sweater. "What about this?"

Meg's brow rose high on her forehead. "Where did you say he was taking you for dinner?"

"Um… I'm not sure. The information is on my phone." She rushed over to her bedside table to grab her phone. "It doesn't give the name, just an address." She read it off.

Meg typed it into her phone. "That's not a restaurant. It's an office building. And not just any office building but the renowned Diamond Building."

Alina frowned. Of course he'd want to meet there. After all, he was only meeting with her to discuss the sale of the Stirling Apartments. That made her decision of what to wear easy because her attire didn't matter. There would be no dress code where she was going.

"Good. That's decided." Alina clutched the jeans and sweater.

Meg reached out and pulled the clothes out of Alina's grasp. "You can't wear that."

"Why not?" Alina frowned. "You just said it wasn't a restaurant, which means I get to feel comfortable."

"Not if you want to impress this guy."

"I don't want to impress him."

"Yes, you do." Meg's eyes implored her to be reasonable. "Why do you have to be so stubborn?"

"Why would I want to impress the man responsible for taking away my home and the home of my friends?" Yes, she thought of most everyone in that apartment building as her friends, except her stepmother and two stepsisters.

It wasn't that she'd always disliked them. In fact, in the beginning it was quite the opposite. She thought it would be nice to have a mother figure, not that anyone would ever replace her mother, but to have two sisters would be amazing. In the end, it had been an amazing disaster.

"Alina, listen to me. You need this guy on your side. He's the only one that can stop the demolition of the building."

As much as she wanted to argue with her friend, Meg was right. The end was in sight and her options were limited. If there was going to be a Christmas miracle, it would have to come from Mr. Scrooge, er... Mr. Toliver.

With the utmost reluctance, Alina asked, "What do you think I should wear?"

"Let me see." Meg rummaged through Alina's closet.

Hangers rattled together. There were a lot of no's and Alina had a feeling putting her friend in charge of her attire for the evening was a mistake.

All the while Prince laid on her bed, staring at her as though she were a traitor for getting dolled up for the enemy. Or maybe that was her own guilt. But if there was any chance of changing this guy's mind about where he built his highrise, she would do what was necessary for the residents of the past, those of the present and the ones of the future.

Alina was ready to go promptly at seven.

It was already dark out but the inky black sky was clear—the big moon hovered overhead but there were too many lights in Manhattan for her to make out the stars.

A black sedan rolled to a stop in front of the Stirling. The driver got out and opened her door for her. She had no idea when Graham said he'd send a car that it would be chauffeur driven. She'd thought he'd meant he would send a taxi to pick her up. She climbed in. This black high-end sedan with tinted windows was quite a few steps up from a taxi. As her hand ran over the buttery-soft black leather seat, she realized it was way out of her league. With this sort of luxury, no wonder Mr. Toliver couldn't understand how an old building could mean so much to so many people.

She glanced down at her little black dress, the one she'd almost refused to wear. She was thankful Meg had been so insistent on her dressing up. Like it or not, if she wanted Mr. Toliver to take her seriously, jeans and a casual sweater weren't going to do the trick.

And maybe some inside information would help. "Excuse me."

"Yes, ma'am," the driver said.

"Do you drive regularly for Mr. Toliver?"

"Yes, ma'am. We should be there in five minutes."

"Thanks. But what I was wondering is, what is Mr. Toliver like?" She had no idea if the driver would speak to her about his employer, but it was worth a try because time was running out before everyone at the Stirling was out on the street.

"Mr. Toliver is the best boss I've ever had."

Now, that shocked her. Sure, she expected the man to say something nice about his boss. After all, he had his job to protect, but this man went above and beyond, saying that Graham was the best.

Maybe it was just that the man didn't know Mr. Toliver well enough. "How long have you worked for him?"

"I've worked for him and his family for eleven years."

Okay. So that wasn't the issue. Maybe it was that the man hadn't worked as a driver for anyone else and had no one to compare him to. "And before you became the Tolivers' driver what did you do?"

"I've been a driver since I graduated high school. My father owns a fleet of cars for hire. But once I started driving for the Tolivers, they requested me regularly. And then one day, the Tolivers hired me full-time. I've been with the family ever since. Mr. Graham is good people. Do right by him and he'll do right by you."

Alina was floored. She really wanted some dirt on the man. She wanted every reason to dislike him. After all, he was taking away her home. And then there was this man who was more than willing to sing the man's praises.

But that couldn't be the truth. She'd read some articles online about the Toliver company being ruthless in business. That was the man she needed him to be so they could go to war over the apartment building. So what if the driver had a different view of Toliver. It didn't mean it was the right view.

The car dropped her off in front of the Diamond Building and she stepped out onto the cleared sidewalk. She lifted her head, trying to see the top of the building. It rose higher and higher until the top floors got lost in the night sky. This man owned all of this? Wow.

Not that she was going to let herself be impressed. He owned all of this because he plowed over people's hopes, dreams and homes to be the biggest and the best.

The uniformed guard behind the impressive reception desk directed her to an elevator that took her to the top floor. She'd be lying to herself if she said she wasn't nervous. There wasn't one thing about this evening that didn't lead her to believe this man had untold power, from his fancy chauffeured car to his company's impressive building. But none of that was going to stop her from speaking her mind.

Graham Toliver might have a lot of power and even more money but he needed to be reminded that his actions had consequences. And though she'd much rather be at home watching a romantic comedy on television while eating Chinese takeout on the couch, she would stand here in her rarely worn little black dress and black heels. She would speak her mind. And she hoped he would really hear her.

She could do this. She thought of all the people in the building who were counting on her to save their homes. She had to do this.

The elevator dinged and then the door rolled back to reveal a big white lobby with a crystal chandelier. Whatever this place was, it was meant to impress people. She was impressed. But it wouldn't deter her from fighting for her home—for her family.

There was only one doorway, so she headed toward it. It was a long hallway that opened into a great room. The walls were black and the floor was white marble. It was quite stunning. And she was starting to suspect that she was in the wrong place.

The room was empty except for one long solitary table. But where was Mr. Toliver?

"You came."

The male voice had her turning to the left and there stood Graham Toliver. He was wearing the same charcoal suit and blue shirt that he'd been wearing earlier that day. How was it that he still looked as fresh as he had hours ago? If she'd have worn the same thing all day, it would look utterly disheveled.

And yet Mr. Toliver stood before her looking like he'd just stepped off the pages of a glossy fashion magazine. And for a moment, her mind stuttered. In that moment, she forgot he was the enemy. And for the briefest second, she imagined what it might be like to meet the man for a dinner date. Her heart picked up its pace. Oh, yes, he would make some lady very happy. But it wasn't to be her. Her feet came back down to earth.

"Of course I came," she said, blinking away her daydream. "We have things to discuss."

He approached her. His eyes were dark and unreadable. "Yes, we do. Please come this way."

She wanted to ask him where they were going, but she resisted the urge. She had no doubt it would be his office. His very big, very impressive office where he would try to bulldoze over her with what he needed and what he wanted.

"Come in," he said.

"What is this?" She glanced around.

"This is a conference room. All of the walls are removable so that the top floor can hold everyone in the office. It's where we host guest speakers and hold training seminars. But for tonight, I had them shrink the size of the room. I hope it's adequate."

"It's very nice." She was drawn to the wall of windows.

She gazed out over Manhattan, which at the moment twinkled with all of the city lights. "I don't know how you get any work done here. I'd be staring out the window all of the time."

He moved next to her. He was so close that she could reach out and touch him, not that she would, or anything, but her pulse raced just being so close to him. It was though an energy force pulsated off him.

"It's an amazing view." His voice was deep and rich, sending waves of awareness throughout her body.

She had to concentrate on anything but how her body responded to him. "Too bad you can't see the Christmas tree in Times Square."

"I'm afraid not. I take it you like that sort of thing."

"You mean getting into the Christmas spirit?" When he nodded, she asked, "Doesn't everyone enjoy the holidays?"

"No."

She turned to him and recalled their discussion at the restaurant. "That's right. You hate Christmas?"

"Hate might be a bit strong, but I could live without it." He cleared his throat. "However, that's not what you're here to discuss."

She looked at him, taking in his serious expression. She felt bad for him and his complete lack of holiday spirit. She wanted to dislike this man. After all, he was tearing down her home, but there was a part of her that felt sorry for him. What had happened to him that he'd lost his joy of the season? Or was it possible he'd never been excited about Christmas?

An image of Graham as a little boy flashed in her mind. She just couldn't believe a man who came from a wealthy background would have been deprived on Christmas morning. There had to be a story there, but she resisted the urge to ask him about it.

CHAPTER FOUR

THE ROOM WAS devoid of Christmas decorations. No tree. No twinkle lights. Nothing.

What was up with that? Maybe they didn't have a chance to get them out yet. It was still a few weeks before Christmas. Alina's gaze moved about the room with its immaculate presentation and perfectly arranged wall hangings. It felt cold and sterile.

It was then that she noticed the soft sound of music. She listened closely, expecting it to be a holiday tune. It wasn't. Interesting. Instead, big band music played. It was nice but not what she had been playing on her radio. From now until Christmas, she was listening to Christmas carols 24/7. There was just something about those festive tunes that put an extra pep in her step.

Graham moved to a small table. She followed, finding two black, thickly cushioned chairs placed on opposite ends of the small table. In the center was a white tapered candle. Its flame flickered. And there were two place settings of what looked to be real china. A private dinner for two?

Alina's heart pitter-pattered. Was this the way Mr. Toliver conducted all of his meetings? She doubted it. She didn't see him sitting across a candlelit table from a businessman to discuss a future deal. So why was he treating her different?

Immediately she wondered if he was interested in her. And just as quickly she dismissed the foolish notion. Why would he be interested in her? He didn't even know her. Worst of all, she was standing in his way of demolishing her apartment building. And she intended to keep on impeding his progress as much as possible.

So what was up with this dinner? Was he hoping some candlelight and good food would sway her? Did he think she'd be that easy? If so, he had another thought coming.

"Mr. Toliver—"

"Please call me Graham."

His friendly gesture wasn't going to soften her up. "All right. Graham, I thought you wanted to talk business."

"As a busy man, I multitask." His tone was matter-of-fact. "Since it is my dinnertime, I thought we would eat while we talk."

She didn't know how she felt about sitting down to a meal with the enemy. Still, at last she'd made it past his bulldog of an assistant, who had previously not let her move beyond the reception area. Perhaps some food might make him more congenial.

"Mr.—er, I mean Graham, our business shouldn't take all that long."

"Then we should begin the meal." He signaled to the server standing across the room.

"Please sit down." He pulled out a chair for her.

Part of her was still hesitant, but she knew it wouldn't help her cause. And without changing his mind about his proposed building site, she would be homeless in the new year.

She approached him. "Thank you." As he waited to help push in her chair, she said, "I've got it."

His eyes momentarily widened, but in a blink his reaction faded. "I didn't expect you to make this easy on me, but do we have to spend the evening in constant opposition? You don't even know me well enough to dislike me that much."

It was true. She didn't know anything about him, except what she'd gleaned on the internet. She hadn't even found a current photo of him, just something from when he was in college with long shaggy hair and a beard. Now his thick dark hair was clipped short around the sides with some longer curls on top. And his sun-kissed face was clean-shaven. The images of him then and now certainly didn't look anything alike.

This was the first time she realized how defensive she'd let herself become. She didn't like the thought that she'd changed so much and not for the good.

Maybe that had played a part in the reason she hadn't had a date in quite a while. Not that this was a date. Far from it.

She had been once bitten by her ex and now she was twice shy. People she could rely on—people she could trust—were hard to find. And she certainly didn't trust Mr. Designer Suit with his billion-dollar smile. He would say and do most anything to get her to move. And it wasn't going to happen—not without a fight.

Graham took a seat across the small table from her. Lifting her gaze, she took in his strong jawline, his straight nose and those very observant eyes. She wondered if he'd been studying her, as well.

When he smiled, her stomach dipped. She caught herself just before she smiled back at him. After all, she didn't trust him. Not at all.

Or was it herself that she worried about the most. All it took was for him to smile for her to forget that they were here to do business.

"So why do you have to build where the Stirling stands?" She wanted to get to the heart of the problem, hoping to find an alternative solution.

"You don't waste time getting to the point, do

you?" He stared at her as though not quite sure what to make of her.

"These days I don't have time to waste."

"In that we have something in common."

She honestly didn't see where they had anything in common. She lived in a modest apartment while he sat here in one of the finest buildings in Manhattan—a building she'd heard he owned. And yet he longed for another building—a bigger one—a new one. No, they had no common ground.

"I doubt we have anything in common," she said.

Interest flared in his eyes. "Is that a challenge?"

A challenge? "No. It's a fact."

His gaze narrowed. "Do you know how much time and effort goes into running a business of this size?"

"No."

"I didn't think so or you wouldn't say something so careless."

She paused for just a moment, letting things settle. "I didn't mean to imply you didn't work hard."

"It certainly sounded like it."

She shook her head. This conversation had gotten off track. "Maybe we should get back to the reason I'm here."

His jaw visibly tightened as a tense silence filled the air. Then he nodded. "If you think that by us having this meeting means I'll change my mind about the fate of the Stirling, it isn't going to happen."

She didn't like that he could read her thoughts. She let his words hang in the air without a response. And then she once more asked, "Why do you have to tear down the Stirling?"

He leaned back in his chair and crossed his arms. "Not that I owe you an explanation, but my company already owns some of the surrounding properties."

"So you figured why not buy more and level the place?"

"It's a matter of using assets to their full value."

As she looked at him, she noticed there was something else in his eyes. Was that sorrow? Or perhaps regret? She couldn't be certain.

And what did he mean by their full value? She considered asking for clarification, but she already knew enough about him to realize he wouldn't be very forthcoming.

Just then the server returned with crystal stemware filled with shaved ice topped with a half dozen jumbo shrimp, a lemon wedge and cocktail sauce. It wasn't until it was in front of her that she realized she hadn't stopped to eat since that morning.

And then the rumble of her stomach filled the air. The heat of embarrassment swirled in her and rushed to her face, setting her cheeks on fire. She hesitated to eat, even if her mouth watered just looking at the food.

"Go ahead." Graham unfolded his white linen napkin. "Eat."

He didn't have to tell her twice. She was so hungry she could have woofed down the appetizer in no time, but she mustered her restraint, not wanting to give Graham a bad impression of her.

Between courses, Graham said, "Why are you fighting so hard to save an old building? That place quite honestly could use some updating."

Her mouth opened but her mind was unable to keep up with her rapidly firing fragments of outrage. She pressed her lips together as she formulated a cohesive response. "It's more than an old building. And what you might call flaws, I call charm."

"I know it's your home now, but that doesn't mean you can't make a home somewhere else."

Before she could respond, their salads and fresh baked bread were served. They quietly ate but all the while her mind was spinning so much so that she didn't even notice what she was eating.

She had to convince Graham that the Stirling

was so much more than brick and mortar. But how? And why would he think that homes were so easily interchangeable? Was that the way all rich people thought?

Alina's fork hovered over her salad plate. "The Stirling is irreplaceable. It is full of family and friends."

"Nothing that can't be found somewhere else."

She inwardly groaned. He wasn't hearing her, not the way she needed him to hear her. If her words weren't enough, she needed to show him what the Stirling meant to her and its residents.

"Is that how you feel about your home?"

He took a sip of ice water. When he returned the stemmed glass to the table, he said, "I like where I live, but if there was a compelling reason to move, I'd do it without making a big deal out of it."

She looked at him in disbelief. "I think it's easier said than done."

"Are you doubting me?" His eyes challenged her.

She leveled her shoulders and lifted her chin ever so slightly. "I am."

His brown eyes grew dark as a muscle in his cheek twitched. "You presume to know me, but I don't care how much you've read about me, you still know nothing about me."

But that wasn't exactly true. She could see that

he was a man who rose to a challenge. It was knowledge she intended to use to her advantage.

The main course consisted of a pasta dish served with marinara sauce and topped with fresh herbs. On the side was chicken parmesan with a thin but crispy coating and some steamed vegetables. It looked delicious and tasted even better.

As she savored each delectable bite, she considered how to open Graham's eyes to the fact that the Stirling was so much more than an old building—more than a hitch in his plans.

When she could eat no more, she pushed aside her plate. It was then that she glanced over at Graham. She noticed he didn't seem interested in his food as he moved it around his plate. He appeared lost in his thoughts.

"Thank you for the meal," she said. "It was very good."

"This was a mistake." Graham balled up his napkin and tossed it on the table.

"What do you mean? The meal?"

"All of it. I thought we could conclude our business over a friendly dinner but obviously that was a miscalculation." Graham stood. "I think we should conclude our business in my office."

She welcomed the excuse to get away from this cozy candlelit dinner. Because even though the room was quite large, Graham's larger than life presence made it feel so much smaller.

Alina nodded in agreement. She folded her napkin and then set it on the table. She noticed that he didn't wait for her as he took long strides toward the exit.

They went down one floor and it was a totally different atmosphere. Instead of being black and white, the foyer was done up in earth tones and royal blue carpet to muffle footsteps. A large reception area sat directly in front of the elevator. On the wall were gold letters that spelled out GH Toliver Investments.

He moved to the right and held open a glass door for her to pass by. And then he led her to the office at the end of the hallway. When he swung open one of the two oversize wooden doors, she wasn't sure what to expect, but it wasn't to find his desk stacked with files. When she looked to the side, there was a long table. It, too, was piled with files.

"I'm sorry for the disheveled appearance," he said. "Since I've taken over, there has been a lot to review and my father was old-fashioned, preferring paper files."

He walked ahead of her, picked up a hefty stack of manila folders and clipped papers and placed them on the table. He returned to his desk. "There. That's better."

She sat down in front of his desk, while he took a seat in a large black leather chair. She didn't like the way she felt at a disadvantage now because her chair seemed shorter than his and a large desk sat between them. She remained perched on the edge of the chair, trying to decide if she should stand.

She wanted this man to take her seriously. After all, this was a very important matter, not just to her but to everyone who lived at the Stirling. Those people were the ones that brought her chicken soup when she didn't feel well and celebrated her birthdays with her. They'd unofficially adopted her after her father passed on and she would do anything for them.

"Mr. Toliver—"

"I thought we were past standing on ceremony."

"There's a lot at stake here and I want you to take me seriously."

"And I won't do that if you call me Graham?"

She narrowed her gaze on him. Why was he making this so difficult? If he was trying to distract her, it wasn't going to work. She had an idea in mind, one that had come to her at dinner after learning a bit about her enemy. A sexy one but an enemy all the same.

She swallowed hard as she prepared to start again. "This matter is very serious for the both of us. You have a building that you want to build. And I have homes I want to save."

Graham rested his elbows on the desk and leaned forward. "And how do you propose we resolve this matter?"

"It's obvious that both of us can't have our way."

"Agreed. You know I'm offering a generous bonus if all of the tenants agree to move out at the beginning of the year. And for that to happen, I need *you* to agree to it."

Her heart clenched. To agree to his plan would mean this would be the last Christmas in the place that had always been her home. "Why me?"

"Because my investigator says that people follow your lead. And from what I witnessed this morning, I would agree. I also know you led the protest here at the office—"

"The protest you avoided."

"I was caught up in important meetings all day, but that doesn't mean I wasn't informed of the disruption."

Disruption? Well, she supposed he could have called it something worse. But it also didn't escape her that she was situated in a very strategic position. She slid back on the chair until the cushion touched her lower back. All the while, she worked up the courage to lay down a challenge—a challenge Graham wouldn't be able to turn down.

"What is it?" His voice interrupted her thoughts.

She focused on him. The idea hovered at the forefront of her mind. Even if he was motivated to win a challenge, there was a distinct possibility he'd turn her down. But if she didn't take this chance—if she didn't challenge him—she didn't have a backup plan.

"Just say it," he said. His gaze searched hers as though trying to figure out what she was thinking.

He was wasting his time trying to guess her thoughts because she scarcely believed what she had come up with. "I'll make you a deal."

His eyes momentarily widened. "You want to renegotiate my very generous offer to have the Stirling tenants move out early?"

"Yes." She hoped her voice sounded more confident than she felt.

There was a noticeable pause. "I'm listening."

Inside she secretly cheered. She'd hooked his interest. "You'll pay for everyone's moving expenses."

"And why would I do that?"

"To get my help. I don't come cheaply."

He leaned forward, resting his elbows on the desk. "I'm figuring that out." He paused as though considering the pros and cons of the suggestion. "You drive a tough bargain. But you have a deal."

"Not so fast. You haven't even heard my final condition."

A muscle in his jaw flexed. He steepled his fingers together as his laser-sharp focus zeroed in on her. "You're pushing your luck."

She knew it, but she couldn't stop now. She leveled her shoulders and met his stare. "Do you want to hear my final condition or not?"

He visibly swallowed as the muscles of his neck moved. "And what would that be? A penthouse for you?"

"Um, no. But now that you mention it…" Suddenly a smile pulled at her face. She couldn't help it. If she didn't hurry with this, she was going to break out into an embarrassing fit of nervous giggles and any chance of making her idea a reality would be lost. And so she rushed to get out her unheard-of demand. "Forget the penthouse. I want you to work for me until Christmas."

A deep frown came over his face. "If you aren't going to take this seriously—"

"I'm very serious. I need to pick up extra shifts at the café and I don't have time to do everything."

"And you want me to do what?"

"I want you to be the building manager."

His eyes widened. "You mean with a toolbox, wrench and such?"

She struggled not to laugh at the look of horror on his face. "Exactly. If a tenant has a problem, you fix it, or if it's too big, you call in experts."

"It surely can't be that much work that you can't handle it in the evenings."

"That's the thing. With this being the busiest time of the year at the café, I'm working a lot of hours. I don't have the extra time like I normally do."

He shook his head as he sat back in his chair. "I don't think you understand. I'm the CEO of a large company. I don't have time to play janitor."

"It's building manager."

"Whatever." He waved off her correction. "The point is I don't have time."

If she didn't do something quick, she was totally going to lose him. "So what you're saying is that you can't do the job."

"That's not what I said." Frown lines creased his brow.

"I bet you don't even know how to work a wrench."

He sat up straighter. "I hate to disappoint you, but I do."

It was her turn to be surprised. She struggled to keep it from showing on her face. "Good. Then you don't have a reason not to agree." And then she reinforced the challenge by saying, "That is, unless you think it'd be too much for you."

He frowned as he crossed his arms. If he was going to outright refuse, he would have done it by now, right? So was he actually considering her totally off the wall idea? And if he did accept, would the people in her building agree with her actions? She hoped so.

Seconds passed in utter silence.

It was though a wall had gone up in his eyes, blocking her attempts to get a glimpse of his inner thoughts. So much for the eyes being the windows to one's soul.

He leaned forward. "I need a day or two to consider this."

Wow! Maybe it wasn't such an outrageous idea, after all.

She hesitated, not wanting him to know just how excited she was to have him take her proposition seriously. "Okay, then. I'll wait to hear from you. I should be going."

He walked her to the elevator. All the while, she wasn't sure what to make of him. Was he really going to consider her offer? Or was he just stringing her along?

When the elevator door slid open, she turned to him. "Thank you for dinner. And the view. I loved the view."

He surprised her with a smile. It lit up his eyes

and made him look younger and sexier, if that was possible. His gaze lowered to her lips. "It is a spectacular view."

And suddenly she had the distinct impression they weren't talking about the same thing. Was he considering kissing her? Her heart pitter-pattered faster as she grew warm. They definitely weren't talking about the same thing at all.

If she didn't step on that elevator right this moment, she had the feeling things would spin completely out of control. And she'd done so well negotiating with him. She refused to falter now for what? A moment of desire? A quick flirtation?

"G-good night," she stammered as she forced her feet to move.

"I'll be seeing you soon." His deep voice sent a wave of anticipation humming through her body.

The elevator door swished shut. She pressed the button for the ground floor. What had happened? One moment they were negotiating a business arrangement and the next moment it was like he was considering kissing her good night. Or had she imagined the whole thing?

CHAPTER FIVE

HIS DAY STARTED before the sun.

The truth was Graham had tossed and turned most of the night. His thoughts had been filled with memories of his dinner with the intriguing Miss Martin. The evening had not gone at all as he'd expected.

After giving up on sleep, he grabbed a hot shower. He leaned against the tile wall as steamy jets beat against his sore muscles. Trying to undo the tangled mess his father had left him at the office was taking its toll on him. And the last thing he needed was this very bizarre agreement with Alina.

When the water started to cool off, he got out of the shower, dressed and headed up to his office. The one thing about taking over his father's city apartment was that it was in the same building as his office.

He was determined to answer some of his emails before the workday officially began and new emails started to flood his in-box. It was tough for him to concentrate on the business at hand as Alina's alluring beauty kept stealing away his thoughts. What was it about her that captivated him so much? She wasn't the first beautiful woman to cross his path. Still, there was something wholly unique about her that drew his attention.

Maybe it was Alina's spunk. She was certainly feisty—

"Good morning." Mary Barnes, his dependable assistant, entered his office wearing a friendly smile. "It looks like you've gotten a jump start on the day."

"Morning." He gazed at the older woman over the top of his monitor. "I have a lot to do today and wanted to get an early start."

Mary shook her head as she laid a stack of paperwork in his in-box. "You work too hard."

"I have to right now. You, of all people, know that."

"Your father certainly left you in a bind, but do you have to do so much on your own?"

"I can't lose the faith of the board."

She nodded. "I understand. If there's something else I can do to help, just let me know."

The decision he owed Alina weighed on his mind. He liked a challenge in business and his personal life. It kept life interesting. It'd been a long time since he met a woman who didn't agree with everything he said.

"What would you say if I told you I was going to work away from the office for a few weeks?"

The woman's eyes momentarily widened. She glanced down at the signed contracts she'd withdrawn from his outgoing basket. "You're going on vacation?"

"Hardly." He paused, realizing if he were going to do this, he would need her help. "I have some delicate negotiations to take care of."

"But you have a meeting with legal next week that you can't miss. And the acquisitions team has been calling every day for an opening in your schedule."

She was right. He couldn't just stop working from now until Christmas. It was impossible. Still, to save the company money in the long-term and to earn the board's respect, he needed to get the residents of the Stirling to move. The sooner, the better. The other buildings in the vicinity had already been vacated. The Stirling was the last holdout.

His father had always talked of one day building a permanent home for Toliver Investments on that site. His father hadn't lived long enough to bring his dream to life but Graham would do it. Toliver Tower would be built upon the land where his father was born and raised. Graham had visited his grandmother in a building adjacent to the

Stirling when he was young. He'd played with the neighbor kids just like his father had done.

"Is there any reason I can't hold the meetings with legal and acquisitions via video?"

Mary opened her mouth to say something, but without uttering a word, she closed it.

"In this day and age of technology," he continued, "I don't see why I can't work remotely. After all, you'll be here to scan whatever mail or documents I need to see."

"Are you sure you're willing to take a step back?"

"No." His voice was firm. "I still intend to be on top of everything. And I will be in the office, just not every day all day long."

Mary arched a brow as she cast him a doubtful look. "If you can do it, I think some time away from this place would do you good. You work too hard."

"But you'll help me see that nothing falls through the cracks?"

She again nodded. "I'll do my best. Shall I start canceling your in-person meetings and make arrangements to move them to video calls?"

"Not yet. But I'll let you know."

He didn't like the thought of stepping back from being in the office because Mary was right, running the business remotely just wasn't the same. And he was a man who liked to be in control of everything.

However, now that he had a plan to make this outlandish idea work, he had to make a decision. But what should it be? Stay in the office and accept the costly delay in the building plans? Or take Alina up on her offer?

One very slow day passed.

Alina spent the time organizing a meeting of the tenants, including her stepmother. It was the first time in Alina's life that her stepmother sided with her about anything. But when her stepmother learned the size of the bonus for moving out early, she was all for it. The catch was they *all* had to agree to move early in order to receive the bonus.

There were heated discussions, but in the end Mr. Merryweather, who was like a grandfather to her, and Mr. Jackson, a talented musician, were the firm holdouts. However, when Alina pleaded with them and told them she had a plan, they said they trusted her. In the end, the plan was a go on her end. However, she hadn't heard back from Graham.

Day two dragged on.

As Thursday evening settled in, blanketing the world in darkness, there still was no word from Graham. Thank goodness for the glow of twinkle lights. They buoyed Alina's spirits. Miracles didn't always happen overnight. Sometimes they took time. However, it didn't make the wait any easier.

Alina had worked the breakfast shift that day as well as coordinated an afternoon Christmas party. Now she was home, pacing the floor. She'd checked her phone off and on all day. It looked like he wasn't even going to have the decency to phone her and turn down her proposal. She groaned in frustration.

Knock-knock.

How was she going to tell the people she cared about that their last chance to save the building was gone? Defeat weighed heavy on her. Now she was out of options. And she had no idea how to tell any of them, not after she'd pleaded with them to give her plan a chance.

Knock-knock.

"Coming." Alina drew in a steadying breath before heading for the door. She glanced through the peephole but couldn't see the person's face, just part of a shoulder.

"Who's there?"

"Graham."

Graham? At this hour? What did it mean?

She unlocked the door and swung it open. "What are you doing here?"

His eyes momentarily widened. "Not exactly the greeting I was expecting."

"Sorry. I just didn't expect to see you. Here. Now. This evening." Oh, she was rambling and making a fool of herself.

"Can I come in?"

Heat swirled in her chest. If she'd have known he was coming to visit, she would have cleaned up. As it was, her dinner dishes were stacked in the sink and her party planning papers for the café were scattered over the couch and coffee table. But what choice did she have?

She backed up, pulling the door wide open. "Sure. Come on in."

When he stepped into her living room, it suddenly seemed to shrink. *Oh, my, this guy is tall.* Her mouth went dry.

She closed the door and then rushed over to the couch and started to collect her papers into a pile. She would sort them out later.

"I... I was working," she said, not wanting him to think she was always this messy.

"I'm sorry for just dropping by. I just out at a business dinner when I realized I left your phone number at the office."

"Oh." She gestured to the two armchairs across from the couch. "Please have a seat."

Still wearing his coat, he moved to the armchair and perched on the edge. He obviously didn't intend to stay long.

Just then her cat entered the room and sauntered straight up to Graham. Prince jumped up on the arm of the chair and stared at Graham, who stared back at him.

"Is he friendly?" he asked.

"Oh, yes. Prince loves everyone."

Graham reached out to pet him. Prince hissed and ran away.

"Prince," she called. The cat kept walking. "Prince, come here." His ears didn't even twitch as he disappeared down the hallway to the bedroom. He always did have selective hearing. If it was time to eat, he heard everything, otherwise he was likely to ignore her admonishments. Alina turned back to Graham. "I'm so sorry. He never acts like that. He really is a nice cat. I swear."

The look in Graham's eyes said he didn't believe her. He cleared his throat. "I've given your proposal serious consideration."

The crucial moment was at hand. The breath caught in her chest. Her mind said that he was going to turn her down, but her heart hoped he wasn't a cold, calculating businessman.

His steady gaze met hers. "And I've decided to take you up on it."

"You did? I mean, that's great." She hoped.

"The reason it took me so long to get back to you was that I had to push the agreement through legal."

Legal? He had his lawyers weigh in on their

arrangement? Just then he withdrew some folded papers from his inner jacket pocket. Why was she surprised? Everything to him came down to looking out for what was best for his company.

Graham held out the papers. "They're just waiting for your signature."

She accepted the papers and stared at them. When she'd proposed the arrangement, she never thought he would take it this seriously.

He leaned back in the chair. "If you want your attorney to look over it, that's fine. But I can promise you it's straightforward."

As she looked at the agreement, she found it was only two pages long and on the second page was Graham's signature.

"Alina, it's okay—"

She held up her finger for him to pause. She started to read it, line by line. And she was surprised to find the language was indeed straightforward, so much so that she could easily understand it. There was nothing in it they hadn't discussed. And the agreement ran from tomorrow through Christmas Eve.

Alina reached for a pen on her coffee table. She signed her name and handed it over. "So you'll be here tomorrow morning?"

He nodded.

"But you realize you'll need to stay here." When his eyes widened in surprise, heat infused her cheeks. "Not here. Not in my apartment. I... I meant here at the Stirling."

He leaned forward, resting his forearms on his thighs. "Where exactly do you envision me staying?"

She couldn't let him back out now. Sure, they signed a formal agreement, but she was certain Graham's legal team could get him out of it. "All of the units are currently occupied. But there's the building manager's office. It has a bed in the back as well as a small bathroom."

He leaned back in the chair as though her words had knocked him off balance. "You're serious, aren't you?"

"Well, you live too far away with the congestion of city traffic. If a pipe bursts or there's a real emergency, you should be close by." And she needed him to spend some serious time here so he would get to know the residents and learn how special Stirling and its inhabitants were to her.

He hesitated. Was he trying to figure out how to back out of this unusual arrangement? Her body tensed as she waited for his next words.

"Fine. I'll be back in the morning." He got to his feet to leave.

The morning? That didn't give her long to make the manager's office presentable, but then again it was small, so there wasn't much to clean.

She glanced up in time to see Graham headed for the door. "Wait." She rushed after him. "Before you go, I should take you around to meet everyone."

"Everyone?"

"Sure. There's sweet Mrs. Hanasey in 504 with her little dog, Louie. And then there is Mr. Jones down in 306. He's always asking for help with his crossword puzzle. Come on. They're anxious to meet you."

"Now?"

"Sure. In the morning, everyone will be rushing around getting ready for work and getting their kids off to school. And we don't want anyone mistaking you for a burglar, do we?"

He hesitated. "I suppose not."

And so they set off to all five floors, knocking on door after door. Most people were hesitant but no one was hostile. Thankfully her stepmother and stepsisters had departed on vacation. Hopefully they wouldn't return before Christmas, but then again, they never checked in with her.

When they stopped outside the building manager's office, Graham turned to her. "Are you going to show me my new home?"

She resisted the urge to worry her bottom lip. If she were to show him that office in its current disheveled state, she was certain he'd bolt for the door. And she wouldn't blame him.

"I... I don't have the key on me." It was the honest truth.

"Well, it is getting late. It can wait until the morning."

"Sounds like a plan." She smiled at him. "You should go. After all, you having packing to do." And she had to make the office homey or at least as welcoming as possible. Was that even possible?

"You're right." Standing in front of her, his gaze met hers. It lingered a moment longer than necessary, making her heart race. "Good night."

Alina swallowed hard. "Night."

It was the only word she trusted herself to say. She worried her voice would betray the way his nearness caused her body to heat up with desire. Not that she was planning to act on those urges. After all, he was the enemy. She couldn't forget that fact.

CHAPTER SIX

AGAINST HIS BETTER JUDGMENT, he'd agreed to Alina's outlandish request.

And ever since, Graham had been working to streamline his business interactions using Mary as his point person in the office. In the end, he'd had to tell his key people the truth about negotiating an early vacancy of the Stirling—just not the whole truth about being the building janitor. His pride refused to divulge it.

Still, people were impressed he was willing to take this important project on himself and not assign it to an underling. He was certain if they knew the details of his agreement with Alina, they wouldn't be impressed at all.

With his earpiece in place, ready to pick up all of his office calls, Graham's chauffeur-driven sedan pulled to a stop outside the Stirling. It was Friday morning at precisely seven a.m. Exactly on time. This was a good way to start things.

On his way in the door, he got precisely three suspicious looks, one *hello* and one *so you really came back* comment. He stopped at the building manager's door. He tried the doorknob but it was locked. Time to visit Alina. There was an added bounce to his step as he headed for the elevator.

However, when he found the elevator was stopped on the top floor, he headed back down the hall and took the steps to the third floor. With his luggage in hand, he paused in front of Alina's door. He couldn't help wondering if he'd made the right decision to go along with her plan. Not giving himself time to answer the question, he knocked on the door.

A moment passed before Alina answered, surprise written all over her pretty face. He glanced down, making sure in his rush he hadn't put on mismatched shoes. Nope. They matched. And he had on pants, a shirt and a coat. He'd remembered everything, even though he'd been distracted all morning with thoughts of seeing her again. Although not in a romantic way, of course.

He raised his gaze. "You look surprised to see me. I did get the time right, didn't I?"

"You did. I… I guess I'm just surprised you're really going through with this."

His brows scrunched together. "Have you changed your mind? Because we have a signed agreement."

She shook her head. "We're good. Come in."

He entered her apartment, dropping his bag

by the door. With the morning sun streaming in through her living room windows, the rays bounced off the Christmas decorations, from a snowman wearing a red scarf that was situated on an end table to a crystal bowl in the center of the coffee table filled with shiny red ornaments. The more he looked around, the more he realized the whole room was decked out for the holidays.

"I've done a little decorating," she said.

"A little?" The words popped out of his mouth before he could stop them. It looked like a lot of decorations to him. What else could she possibly add?

As though reading his thoughts, she said, "It's still missing the Christmas tree, but with trying to balance two jobs, I haven't had time to get one." She gestured for him to wait a moment. "Let me grab my shoes and I'll show you where you'll be staying."

While she finished getting ready, he continued to glance around the apartment. The furniture was old but it was well cared for. The modest living room and kitchen were a bit crowded but otherwise orderly. He wondered if they were always this way or had she gone to the extra effort because she knew he'd be showing up. No, of course she wouldn't. She didn't seem to care what he thought of her—and maybe that was what held his interest.

"I'm ready." Alina approached the door.

He joined her there. When he drew near her, he inhaled a light scent of berries and champagne. It was an interesting combination. Before he could breathe in that intoxicating scent again, she exited the apartment. Disappointment assailed him.

He followed her to the elevator. She was quieter than she'd been in the past, but then again, she'd gotten what she'd wanted—him agreeing to play along with her plan—but if she expected this arrangement to change his mind about tearing down the Stirling, it wasn't going to happen. The tower and all it implied was just too important.

She pressed the down button and immediately the door slid open. He stepped inside, noticing just how small the elevator was compared to the bank of elevators at the Diamond Building where the Toliver offices were located.

Though rumor said that the Tolivers owned the Diamond Building, they didn't. And with the building fully occupied, there was no space for the company to expand. As it was, they had employees doubling and tripling in offices. It was getting bad. They needed the new building up and operational as soon as possible.

As the silence dragged on, Graham grew uncomfortable. He said the first thing that came to mind. "I wonder if there's enough work around here to necessitate me living here."

A knowing smile lit up her face. "You'll see."

Before he could respond, the elevator stopped, the door squeaked open and Alina was on the move again. She paused outside the building manager's office and inserted the door key. And then she swung open the door.

"Home sweet home." She stepped aside, letting him enter first.

He wasn't sure what he was expecting, but it certainly wasn't this. There were no windows in this room. Just one solitary light fixture overhead, which didn't illuminate the room all that well.

The gray walls were bare. There was an old metal desk with a few dings on the side. Though it had been cleaned off, probably by Alina, it was still not welcoming. It was about half the size of his sleek new desk at his office. There would definitely have to be some adjustments made if he were to work here, and he most definitely needed to work while he was here.

"I know it's not much," Alina said, "but I've moved most of the clutter to this big walk-in closet."

He turned around to find a door behind him. He followed Alina inside. A single light bulb hung overhead, illuminating two stepladders, a hot water tank, a couple of shelving units with some home improvement items and an assortment of other items.

"You weren't kidding about me being the building janitor—"

"Building manager," she corrected. "Most everything you'll need should be here. If not, let me know and we can work something out."

"I think I can manage."

"There's one more room to show you." Alina moved to the back of the unit and opened the door. "This is your bedroom."

As he stepped into the room, he noticed the minimal furnishings. Beneath a window was a twin bed and next to it was a nightstand with a lamp. Wait. A twin bed?

He hadn't slept in a bed that small since he was a kid. And to make matters worse, there was a pink comforter with large white polka dots. The pillow propped up against the headboard had a pink pillowcase with a unicorn. He inwardly groaned. He felt like he'd just stepped into a girl's dormitory.

"I know it's not fancy like what you're accustomed to, but I can assure you the entire place is clean. When some of the residents found out what I was doing, they offered to help."

He drew in a deep breath, smelling a fresh lemony scent. That should have made him feel better, but he still was having a very hard time adjusting to the accommodations. This wasn't going to do. Not at all. Not for a few weeks. Not even for a few days.

Yet he kept his thoughts to himself. He didn't want to insult Alina after the trouble she'd gone to. But hopefully she wouldn't mind him making this unit his own. After all, he did own the building. And he wasn't accustomed to asking anyone's permission to do as he pleased. He didn't plan to start now.

He stepped toward the small bed, barely big enough for his six-foot-three frame. He settled his bag on the end of the bed, causing the comforter to become disheveled. When he went to straighten it, he noticed it was double-sided. The bottom side was gray. Thank goodness. He'd flip it over, problem solved.

Ring-ring-ring.

Graham turned to Alina.

"It's the phone on the desk," she said. "I can get it for you."

He was tempted to take her up on her offer, but he said he would do this and he refused to break his word. "I'm on it."

He didn't even want to imagine what problem awaited him. He picked up the phone with a friendly hello. The conversation was short and straight to the point. There was no small talk, just the problem laid out. Was this how his next few weeks were going to be?

"Yes, Mr. Merryweather. I'll be right there." Graham hung up the apartment phone.

"What did he want?" Alina asked.

"It appears there's a leak in his bathroom."

A smile came over Alina's face and though Graham already thought she was beautiful, when she smiled, it took his breath away. There was something about this woman that was very special.

"What are you smiling about?" He wondered if he had some breakfast stuck in his teeth.

"Nothing."

"It's something."

"It's just that I never imagined a big CEO like you would be willing to fill in as the building maintenance guy." She glanced at her fitness tracker. "I don't have much time before I have to leave for work, but I can go with you."

"Don't worry. I've got this."

He hoped. He wasn't going to mention that he'd been guided to YouTube videos by his assistant. When he'd checked it out, he'd found they had how-to videos on most every subject. He just hoped the tutorials were enough.

"Okay. If you don't need anything else, I should be going." She started for the door before turning back. "Oh, I forgot. You'll need this."

When she handed over the key, their fingers touched. Her skin was warm and soft. His gaze met hers. There was a spark of emotion in her blue eyes—cornflower blue like the flowers in the sunny field, a place where you could lose track of time—and he could easily get lost in her beautiful eyes. She withdrew her hand and the connection was broken.

As she walked away, he stood in the doorway staring at her retreating form as though hypnotized by the gentle sway of her hips. It wasn't until she stepped out of sight that he snapped out of his trance. He gave himself a mental jerk. He couldn't let himself get distracted—no matter how sweet the distraction.

CHAPTER SEVEN

WHAT HAD HE been thinking?

He shouldn't be here. Being a building manager was way outside of his skill set. How Alina managed it all plus her work at the café was truly impressive. Thankfully his very first job was really quite easy and no YouTube video was necessary. All it took was a few turns of the wrench.

Graham carried the red toolbox into the living room. "All fixed."

"Thanks," Mr. Merryweather said from his spot on his brown recliner, a sports station playing on the television while he held a book in his hands. "I used to be able to do those things but I can't get down on my knees the way I used to."

"No problem."

Mr. Merryweather gazed at him over his reading glasses. "You taking over the maintenance job from Alina?"

"Only temporarily. She's busy working holiday parties at the restaurant."

Mr. Merryweather nodded. "Glad to hear she'll be back."

"Why's that?"

"She always has time to talk." *Wasn't that what he was doing now?* Mr. Merryweather continued. "And she usually brings a treat?"

"A treat?"

Mr. Merryweather nodded again. "She makes the best cookies."

The man really thought he was going to take time out of his busy day to bake? Not a chance. "Sorry. I don't bake."

Mr. Merryweather's face grew serious as his bushy white brows drew together. "Because you're too busy kicking people out of their homes."

Ouch. This man certainly wasn't worried about pulling his punches. Was that why Alina had smiled when he'd told her who was on the phone?

Regardless, he still needed to get through to the man. "Mr. Merryweather, wouldn't it be nice to get a new place? Maybe one where the plumbing is updated?"

Hmph! "The plumbing here is just fine. And the name is Merryweather."

"That's what I said, Mr. Merryweather."

The man sighed. "There's no mister. It's just Merryweather."

"Okay, Merryweather. I'm no expert but even I can see that the building needs some work."

Right then Graham's earpiece buzzed, signaling an incoming call. But whoever it was would have to wait. This conversation was important.

Merryweather frowned at him. "Just because things get old doesn't mean they should be disregarded."

Graham opened his mouth and then promptly closed it. He wondered what it'd take to get the man on board with the sale. Because Graham was beginning to realize he was going to have to win over the tenants one at a time.

"You could pick out wherever you want to move." Graham's gaze moved to the television. "Maybe somewhere close to sporting events so you could see them in person instead of having to watch them on television."

"I like my television. I can see the game better than if I were there in person."

It seemed as though Mr. Merryweather—er, Merryweather—was determined to argue with him, no matter what Graham said. The best thing for him to do now was to pick up his red toolbox—er, Alina's red toolbox—and head out the door.

"I should be going," Graham said.

"You won't be back, right?"

What? That was a strange comment. "Not unless you call."

"No. I mean, next time Alina will come to do the work, right?"

"I'm going to be filling in for Alina until Christmas."

"Oh." Talk about a deflated sound.

Graham shifted his weight from foot to foot. He couldn't help but wonder if this was what his employees thought with him stepping in to fill his father's place at the helm of the company. He didn't do things like his father had done for many years. And he knew it bothered a lot of employees.

However, his father's resistance to change had put the company in a bind. There was no room to grow. And building a new home for Toliver's was the only way to secure its future.

"What if I were to bring a treat the next time I visit?"

Interest lit up the older man's face. "What sort of treat?"

Graham didn't realize details would be necessary. "What would you suggest?"

"Well, I don't know. You're the one that mentioned it."

Technically, Merryweather had been the first to mention a treat. This was all Alina's fault. Whoever heard of a handyman bringing baked goods to the tenants? Wasn't it enough to fix whatever may be broken? Leave it to Alina to raise the bar. No wonder no one wanted to move.

"How about sugar cookies?" Graham suggested. "After all, it's the holiday season."

"No. Alina bakes the best sugar cookies."

Graham sighed because the big toolbox was growing heavy and he didn't want to put it down as that might signal he was staying for a while and that wasn't the case.

"I know, gingersnaps." Merryweather smiled. "My mother used to make them. They were just right with a punch of flavor and they snapped when you bit into them."

Were those Christmas cookies? Graham wasn't up on his Christmas fare, but then again, did it really matter so long as Merryweather was happy? He just wondered if the Polka Dotted Bakery made them. "Gingersnaps, it is. Goodbye, Mr. Merryweather."

"Tell Alina I said hi."

"I'll do that."

Graham let himself out of the apartment and headed toward the elevator. Then, realizing that every time he stepped in it he could run into a tenant that inevitably needed something done around their apartment, he opted to take the stairs.

But when he opened the fire door and stepped

into the hallway of the first floor, there was an older woman standing outside the building manager's door. He inwardly groaned.

It was probably another tenant that needed help with something or other. And he really didn't have time. He had five reports that needed reviewed and two memos to sign off on. How Alina maintained another job in addition to managing the building was totally beyond him. This position seemed to be full-time and then some—and he'd been here less than two hours!

"Can I help you?" he asked.

The older woman turned to him. Her bright red lips pursed together as her eyes narrowed behind black framed glasses. "Do I know you?"

He didn't recall her from his brief tour the prior evening. But it had gotten too late to meet everyone. "No, you don't."

"Then what are you doing in this building?" And then her gaze lowered to the toolbox in his hand. "You borrowed Alina's toolbox?"

"Worse than that, I'm filling in for the building manager."

"Oh." Her eyes widened. "For a moment, I'd forgotten about Alina's arrangements."

"Do you need something fixed?"

"Come with me." She crooked her finger.

His business would have to wait a bit longer. Perhaps he should have asked Alina more questions before agreeing to her terms. From his point of view, she definitely got the better end of the deal.

He was the sexiest building manager ever.

As soon as the totally inappropriate thought of Graham came to Alina, she dismissed it.

The next morning, Alina couldn't think of Graham as just another man. He was anything but the usual guy that passed through her life and it was more than his devastatingly handsome looks. He held the keys to her future. He decided if she stayed or left—of whether she clung to the makeshift family that had surrounded her through the loss of both of her parents. And it was for that reason she had to keep her wits about her.

Showered and dressed for work, she moved to her bedroom door to find Prince waiting for her. He lifted his head and blinked.

"Mrrrr..."

He got up from his spot at the end of the bed and rubbed over her ankles. Alina bent over and picked him up. Prince stretched his neck, pressing his nose to hers. Alina's heart swelled with love.

She ran her hand down over Prince's back as his deep purr emanated. Holding him with one arm, she opened the door. She carried the still purring Prince to the kitchen, where she lowered him to the floor.

"Mrrrr..."

"Okay, I'm getting your breakfast." She reached in the cabinet and grabbed a can of cat food and one of Prince's bowls.

Once Prince was taken care of, she turned and filled the coffeemaker with water and added a pod. With a press of a button, her morning caffeine was under way. And boy did she need a nice big mug of coffee this morning.

Prince sat next to her as he woofed down his breakfast like he hadn't been fed in days. When the bowl was licked clean, he looked up at her. His eyes begged her for seconds.

"Sorry, buddy, that's all you get. The vet said I had to quit spoiling you." When she bent down to soften her words by scratching behind his ears, he dashed past her. He definitely didn't like his new diet.

Knock-knock.

Alina opened the door to find Graham standing there. "Good morning."

"I need more time."

"Time? Time for what?" She had no idea what he was talking about.

He smiled at her and then pointed at the earpiece. "I don't care what you have to do to make it work. I'm not signing off until I have a chance to review the details. And yes, I know it's Saturday. I have to go." He glanced at her, looking a bit sheepish. "Sorry about that. It was the office."

"Come in. Why are you working on the weekend?"

"Business waits for no man."

She shook her head in disbelief. He needed a break more than she thought. She gave Graham a quick once-over, finding him dressed in jeans and a red sweater. At least it was a change from his designer suits and ties. Although she couldn't decide which look she preferred. He looked good no matter what he wore—

She stopped herself. What was it about being around him that muddled her thinking? She just got done telling herself that she wasn't going to be susceptible to his good looks. This was important. He had to take her seriously.

"Is something wrong?" He glanced down at his outfit, then lifted his head, his brows knitted together in confusion.

"Uh. No, I... I was just thinking that I had to make time to get a Christmas tree before all of the good ones are picked over." She busied herself by pouring him a cup of coffee. "I'm sure you already have your tree."

He accepted the cup. "I told you I'm not a fan of Christmas."

"Oh, that's right." Alina couldn't imagine not

doing anything at all. She loved Christmas. The joy of the season was so infectious. "Not even when you were a kid?"

Graham shrugged. "My father said it was nothing more than a marketing scheme."

"That's so sad because it's so much more. Maybe you'll see it differently this year."

"I don't think so. I have my business to run and it takes up all of my time."

"You know what they say about all work and no play."

He took a sip of coffee. "Are you implying I'm boring?"

She held up both hands in innocence. "I don't even know you yet." Alina filled her to-go coffee mug. "I have to go to work now. Was there anything you needed?"

"I was wondering if you'll be around for dinner." He rushed to add, "It'll be a business dinner as I'm sure I'll have questions about the building."

"Sorry, I'll be late. I'm going to work as many hours as they'll give me throughout the holidays."

"Because of me?"

She busied herself, checking for her keys and purse, in order to avoid his pointed gaze. And then she decided that they couldn't just dance around this subject. She lifted her head and met his gaze straight on. "Yes. Rent in this city is going to cost a fortune. And even with everything I'm saving, I don't know if I can afford to live someplace else. And I have it better than other people in the building who are retired with no means of raising additional income."

He frowned. "I'm giving out bonuses."

"But how far will they go? Let me tell you, not very far at all."

Graham rubbed the back of his neck. "I don't know what to say."

"I don't expect you to say anything. I just need you to understand—really understand—the ramifications of your actions." She shrugged on her red coat. "Is your new building really this important?"

"Yes." Graham's voice was firm.

It was not the answer she wanted to hear. She grabbed her stocking cap, decorated with a design of white snowflakes, from her coat pocket. She couldn't get upset. She had to remain calm. After all, her plan to change his mind had barely begun.

She forced a smile to her lips. "I've got to get going. I'll see you later." Just then Prince returned to her side. She bent down to pet him. "I'll see you later, too. Be good."

Prince turned around to walk away. He paused in front of Graham and looked up at him. Alina would love to know what Prince was thinking.

When Graham noticed, he moved to pet Prince, who once again scurried away. What was up with that? Was it possible Prince was jealous? Laughter bubbled up in her throat.

"It's not funny," Graham said. "He just won't give an inch."

"Hey, he didn't growl at you this time. That's something."

He held up the still full cup. "Mind if I bring this back later?"

"Not at all."

Graham headed for the door, but she was standing between him and the door. As he passed by her, their bodies briefly brushed against each other. Her heart slammed into her chest as awareness set every one of her nerve endings a-tingling. So much for telling herself that she could treat Graham like everyone else.

"I'll see you later," she said as she put the lid on her to-go mug.

"I'll be here."

And then the door closed. She could at last take a full breath. This was going to be a very long few weeks. Very long indeed.

CHAPTER EIGHT

HER FEET ACHED.

Her knees ached.

Her arms ached.

Okay, so there wasn't a part of Alina's body that didn't ache. She'd worked a ten-hour shift. Ten hours of being on her feet, carrying heavy trays of food to table after table, was exhausting. She couldn't wait to get back to her party planning. At least then she'd be seated.

After this very busy week, all she wanted to do on this Friday evening was kick off her rubber-soled shoes and climb in a bubble bath with a couple of candles and a captivating thriller. She wanted to get lost in the pages as the heroine outsmarted the killer.

But when she entered the foyer of her apartment building, she breathed in the most delightful aroma of… What was that? And where was it coming from?

She inhaled again. The scent of oregano and garlic called to her. Her stomach rumbled in response. She'd been too busy at work to stop and eat. But on the plus side, she'd received the biggest tip that night. And it was going straight toward her future rent/deposit.

Graham stepped into the hallway. Upon seeing her, his eyes widened. "You just saved me a trip."

She approached him. "How did I do that?"

"I was headed to your apartment to leave a note on your door."

"About what?"

"Dinner." He went on to tell her that he had had dinner delivered from one of Manhattan's poshest restaurants.

"Wow. I've heard how hard it is to get a table. No one ever said they have delivery service."

"They don't."

"But you—"

"Know the owner."

"Lucky you."

Alina took a step back. "I'll let you eat before it gets cold."

"But I got enough to share. Unless you already ate?"

"There wasn't time. We were too busy."

"Well, come in." He gestured her inside his apartment.

She didn't know what she was expecting to find, but it was though the unit had had a complete makeover. In the past week, he'd certainly made himself at home. There was a new desk with two large computer monitors side by side and a black leather desk chair.

"I hope you don't mind that I made a few changes."

She shook her head, still taking in the changes. "Not at all."

Against the other wall were a couple of comfy-looking chairs and a small fridge with a micro-wave atop it.

"This—" he gestured to the wall behind him "—is for anyone who wants some coffee or doughnuts in the morning."

"So you're having an open-door policy, literally."

"Something like that."

She stared at the small table by the doorway with a new coffeemaker and a big white baker's box with the Polka Dotted Bakery logo. There was only one doughnut left and a bunch of crumbs. Wow. He really had made himself at home. And it looked as though he was trying to win over the Stirling residents, one doughnut and coffee at a time.

"Have a seat." He gestured to the chairs.

"I can help get the food."

"You are my guest. I've got this." He turned and set to work.

The man was certainly stubborn. She looked

on as he pulled out plates and utensils from one bag and food containers from a second bag. She grew uncomfortable with him waiting on her when she was perfectly capable of doing it herself.

"This isn't necessary," she said. "I can do it."

"Yes, it is necessary. You look exhausted."

"I'm fine." *Liar.* "I can help you."

He arched a disbelieving brow and stared at her until she sat down. She stifled a sigh as she got off her feet. Her pride refused to let Graham see that he was right about her needing to sit down.

He made short work of serving up the food. When he handed her a plate, her mouth watered.

Graham sat down. "There. Was that so hard?"

"What?"

"Letting me do something for you?"

She placed the plate on her lap. "I don't know what you're talking about."

"You are always going out of your way to help people, but you refuse to accept help in return."

Heat flared in her cheeks. "I don't need people going out of their way for me. I'm fine on my own."

"How about just letting someone do something nice for you because they want to?"

Had she spent so much of her life waiting on others that she'd learned to ignore her own needs?

She dismissed the thought. Graham was putting wayward thoughts in her very tired brain.

For a few minutes they ate in silence. Alina smothered a moan of delight over the food. "This is delicious."

"So glad you like it. See. It doesn't hurt to let someone do things for you."

"Really?" She couldn't believe what she was hearing. "You make it sound like my being self-sufficient is a fault."

His gaze lowered to his plate. "I'm just saying sometimes you have to consider yourself."

She didn't like the turn in this conversation. It reminded her too much of how her stepmother used to needle her with snide little insults here and there. The food was overcooked, the laundry was too wrinkled—it went on and on.

Her gaze narrowed on him, and she became intent on turning this conversation away from what he viewed as her shortcomings. "All this advice from a man who wrote the book on being stubborn."

"Stubborn?"

She nodded. "You insist on doing things your way."

"This from the woman who refuses to accept that this apartment building is going to be de-molished. Instead of making plans for the future, you're clinging to the past."

Her gaze narrowed on him. "The past is important. And it's not just me that thinks so. Haven't you learned anything by working around the building this week?"

"I've learned that Mrs. Campbell in 203 has a cute little dog that is very curious. I've learned that Mr. Merryweather prefers to be called Merryweather minus the mister. He also has a sweet tooth and he misses your visits. Apparently I'm not nearly as good of company as you. And I know there's some really nosy woman on the first floor that refuses to change her own light bulb. She asked a lot of questions about you."

Alina had a sneaking suspicion she knew who it was. "Did the woman have bleached blond hair?" When he nodded, she asked, "Did she have on a lot of makeup, especially eye makeup?"

"How did you know?"

"Because it was my stepmother. Although I thought she was supposed to be on vacation. I must have gotten my weeks mixed up."

"Your stepmother?" When she nodded, he asked, "Do you two get along?"

Alina rolled her eyes. "Not at all."

"Wow. That bad?" When she bobbed her head, he turned his attention back to his plate of food. "Is she the only family you have?"

"Yes. My father married her after my mother died. He was the building manager—"

"That's how you learned to do everything."

She nodded. "I always followed him around. He showed me how to replace pipes, paint apartments and everything else." When she noticed Graham smiling, she asked, "What's so amusing?"

"I'm just imaging you as a little girl with a wrench in one hand, a hammer in the other and a smidge of grease on your cute little nose."

He thought her nose was cute? She wondered what he thought about the rest of her, but she didn't dare vocalize her thoughts.

She swallowed hard. "That was me. A total tomboy. After some comments from one of the busybodies in the building, my father got it in his head that I needed a female role model—someone to teach me how to be a young lady. And so he married my stepmother."

"I bet you weren't happy about it."

"In the beginning, she seemed nice enough, but once they were married, everything changed."

Why was she telling him all of this? She never talked about her family with anyone. At least, she tried not to, but when they lived in the same building, it made it extremely difficult.

A yawn escaped her. And now with her stomach appeased, her eyelids grew heavy.

"You should go," he said.

"I think you're right. Thank you for dinner. It was delicious."

"You're welcome."

On her way to her apartment, she replayed her dinner with Graham. Had they moved from adversaries to friends?

Because only a friend would order her dinner and from an A-list restaurant no less. And only a friend would wait on her. Then there was their conversation; it was the kind that was far too personal to have with her enemy.

She would have to maintain her distance going forward. Because falling for Graham would be the biggest mistake of her life. All she had to do was look at what he'd done to his temporary home. New furniture. New electronics. And a new coffee machine with daily doughnut delivery.

It was a life far from hers. Hers was so much simpler. So much so that he wouldn't even have bothered with her if it wasn't for their agreement.

CHAPTER NINE

AT LAST A day off.

A morning to sleep without an alarming rousing her. Much to Prince's chagrin.

While lounging in bed, Alina decided how she wanted to spend her Saturday. A big smile pulled at the corners of her mouth. Prince marched up the bed and meowed loud and long.

"Okay. Okay." Alina ran her hand over his head and down his back. "I get it. You're hungry."

She rushed through her morning shower and dressed. She and Prince shared breakfast. He had seafood supreme while she opted for two frozen waffles and juice. As she ate, she thought of her plans for the day and then she got an even better idea—one that would hopefully fill Graham with some holiday spirit.

With her dirty dishes in the sink, she grabbed her purse and coat. She rushed out the door. She was a lady on a mission.

She stopped outside Graham's door. She didn't

have to knock because the door was already open with a sign that said Free Coffee and Doughnuts.

Graham glanced up from his computer, a smile lighting up his face. "Good morning." His gaze momentarily dipped to her outfit before returning to her eyes. "You aren't dressed for work."

"I have the day off. And we have plans."

He tilted his head to the side and looked at her. "Do I even want to ask what you have in mind?"

A smile tugged at her mouth. "Don't you trust me?"

"I don't know. I'm having visions of replacing plumbing or something even worse."

That made her laugh. "What if I told you there were no repairs involved in today's activities?"

"Then I'd ask if you made sure all of the building's residents were on board with your plan."

She couldn't stop smiling and it was all his fault. There was just something about him that made her happy when she was around him. "Stop being so difficult. If someone needs you, they can leave a message. Now grab your coat."

"Not until you tell me where we're going."

His pointed stare let her know that he was serious. She sighed. "Fine, if you must know we're going to get a Christmas tree. It's past time to put it up. And I just can't wait any longer."

"Why me?"

"Because you need some holiday spirit. Don't you want to put up a Christmas tree?"

He shrugged. "I don't know."

"Come on." She headed into the hallway, hoping he would follow. This man needed some Christmas in his heart. And she couldn't think of a better way to start his transformation than by picking out an evergreen.

She slipped on her winter coat. She wanted to glance back and see if Graham was following her lead, but she resisted the urge. She'd done all she could. If he didn't want to have some Christmas fun, she wasn't going to make him. But she would feel bad for him. Who didn't enjoy the holiday festivities?

She'd just pulled on her knit cap when Graham said, "Are you going to just stand there all day? We have to get a Christmas tree."

The smile returned to her face and so did the hope that there would be a Christmas miracle this year—that Graham would find his holiday spirit and her home would be saved.

Christmas tree shopping.

He didn't have time for this.

Graham thought of the budgets he had to review, trying to cover the endeavors his father had obligated the company to participate in while trying to secure the necessary funds to cover the mounting expenses to build Toliver Tower.

He had a plan to bring on a new partner who would take over some of the investments, freeing up Toliver funds. But finding the right partner was difficult. And now that he'd found someone who would be a good fit with Toliver, they were hesitant to commit in the current economic climate.

But he also realized the importance of making Alina happy. She was the key to having the Stirling residents moved out by the beginning of the year. It would give his contractors an extra two months to clear the land so they could be ready to break ground in the spring.

And most of all, she was finally doing something for herself. He hadn't known her for long but it was long enough to know that she truly did put others' needs before her own. Today would be different. He'd see to it.

As they headed out into the cold, crisp morning, Graham couldn't help thinking of his father. He would say buying a Christmas tree was an utter waste of time and money. His priority needed to be on the company and fixing the financial mess he'd inherited.

But Graham's mother would be all sorts of happy to see him doing something that wasn't work related. He thought of calling her. His hand moved to his pocket to grab his phone. *She would be happy to hear from me, wouldn't she?* He hesitated. The last conversation they'd had was harsh and some words were said that just couldn't be taken back.

"What has you so quiet?" Alina said. "Did I pull you away from something important?"

She had but he wasn't going to admit it. "Nothing that can't wait until later."

His response brought a smile to her face and it was then that he knew he'd chosen the right answer. Because when she smiled, it lit up his whole world. He didn't even know something like that was possible. He'd certainly never felt something so intense before. And he had absolutely no idea what to do about it. And so he ignored it—pretended like it had never happened. Like any of that was possible.

"We're almost there," she said.

"Almost where?"

"At the tree lot where I've been getting my Christmas tree since I was a kid."

"That's a really long time. Wouldn't it be easier just to buy an artificial tree?"

She scrunched up her nose. "I know it works for some people. And that's great for them. But I love having a live tree. There's just something about the pine scent and the look of it that really sets off the holiday."

He actually never heard of anyone so enthusiastic about a Christmas tree before. He couldn't help but wonder if she got this excited about everything in her life.

She glanced over at him. "I know you don't celebrate Christmas now but what was it like when you were a kid?"

"My father thought the holiday was a waste of time, but my mother insisted we at least have a small artificial tree. It wasn't much. It sat on a table in our living room. My father sighed every time he looked at it." Graham remembered those days and how he didn't understand how his friends would have these big fancy trees with all of the lights but they only had an itty-bitty tree. "The day after Christmas it went back into storage and life went back to normal."

"Is that what you wanted?"

He didn't want to answer. He didn't like to think about the past. "It doesn't matter. We're here to get you a tree."

She stopped just outside of the tree lot and turned to him. "But it does matter because unless you've decided to give in on our deal, we'll be sharing the holiday season."

Give in? Him? Never. He was in it to win it. Everything was riding on him lowering Toliver's financial obligations and creating space for their growing workforce—something his father put off for far too long.

"Fine," Graham said, "if you must know, back then I wanted a real tree—a tall tree—like my friends had. But it doesn't matter anymore."

"It matters," she said with an understanding tone as though she could see right through him.

He wanted to argue the point but decided it was better not to. He followed her into the tree lot. With it still being early in the season, the lot was filled with trees—to the point where it was difficult to walk down many of the paths.

There were short chubby trees, tall slender ones, short needles, long needles, some greener, some bluer. He honestly never stopped and paid enough attention to realize just how many different types of Christmas trees were available.

He followed Alina around the lot. She paused to give some a closer inspection before moving on. He wondered what she was inspecting but he didn't ask. He didn't want her to get the impression he cared all that much.

Christmas was just another day. Or at least it should be. Instead it was a day where no work got done. A day where his plans to prove himself to his mother, to his board, to the world, were put on hold. If anything, Christmas should be for the children, but let the adults get on with business.

* * *

Alina carried the top of the tree.

Graham held the trunk.

With a light snow falling, they walked home. Not that the tree was heavy. Graham offered a couple of times to carry it all by himself, but she wouldn't hear of it. After a bit of back and forth, they agreed to share the task.

However, now that they were back in her apartment and had the tree set up, Alina realized she might have been a bit overly ambitious when it came to the size. The top of the tree touched the ceiling. It hadn't looked that big in the tree lot. There were lots of other trees that were so much bigger.

And it was wide—very wide. The corner she'd cleared, next to the window, wasn't big enough. The couch had to be moved. Again. And an end table had to be put into her bedroom in order for people to be able to move about the room.

Still, it was a pretty tree. She stopped and stared up at it. It was going to take her stepstool to reach the top. Then again, she might have to borrow the stepladder from the building manager's office, erm, from Graham.

"Do you want me to cut the top off so it fits better?" Graham's deep voice drew her from her thoughts.

She turned to him. "Definitely not. You really

don't know anything about Christmas trees, do you?"

"What's that supposed to mean?"

"That you never cut the top of a tree. If you want to shorten it, you do it from the bottom."

He shrugged. "Same difference."

"No, it isn't. If you cut off the top, it'll look funny. And you won't be able to add the angel."

"Do you want me to cut the bottom?"

She stepped back, taking in the sheer magnitude of the tree. There was no room in her tiny apartment to cut it. They'd just have to make do. "It's good just the way it is."

Graham moved up next to her. "It is?"

"It is. Now we have to decorate it."

He shook his head. "I'm out. I'm no good at that kind of stuff. Besides, I have work to do."

She pressed a hand to her hip. "Don't you ever take a day off?"

"Listen to who's talking—"

"What's that supposed to mean?"

"That you work all of the time. If not at the café, you're working here."

She huffed. She wanted to argue with him, but it was true. She worked as much as she could to save money for her uncertain future. But she didn't want to ruin the day arguing with him over the future of the building because day by day he was beginning to make friends with the residents of the Stirling. But would it be enough to change his mind?

"Okay," she said. "Go do your work. I'm going to turn on some Christmas music?"

He shook his head and headed for the door.

She turned her back to him and started opening the box of decorations closest to her. She lucked out, finding it was the box with the light strands. She plugged them into the wall to make sure they still worked before she started stringing them at the bottom of the tree. It wasn't an easy task when the tree was so large. She couldn't even come close to wrapping her arms around it.

She had made a couple of rounds when she stretched as far as she could to place the bundled light strand on the tree branch before repositioning herself to pass it around the back when her fingers brushed Graham's. Her head jerked up, surprised to find he hadn't left, and their gazes met. A current of attraction pulsed up her arm and set her heart pounding.

Alina shook her head. She'd said too much. This was a subject she never discussed. It was easier just to keep it to herself.

"When my father had a heart attack and passed away, I'd just turned eighteen. I inherited the apartment. My stepmother was furious and took me to court, but it was ruled that the apartment and the rent control lease were rightfully and legally mine. I was hoping it would be the last I saw of that woman and her daughters, but she used the life insurance money to move into a larger apartment in the building."

Graham reached out and gave her hand a squeeze. "I'm sorry you went through all of that. I'm sure you were a great kid."

"Why are you so sure?"

"Because I see how you are with people you care about. You go out of your way for them, from baking cookies to fighting on their behalf to save their homes. It takes a very special person to do those things. Not to mention sharing your Christmas traditions with someone you consider the enemy."

Heat rose in her cheeks. "I never said you were the enemy."

"But you thought it. And I understand because I was in your place, I'd feel the same way. But with all you've been through, did you ever consider moving?"

CHAPTER TEN

THE BREATH STILLED in her lungs.

For a moment, it was though time came to a sudden halt.

Alina stared deeply into Graham's eyes. She could see the future—a future with him in it. She could imagine this was just the first of many Christmases where they'd decorate the tree together. In her daydream, she envisioned him pulling her close and kissing her, not just any kiss, but one filled with passion and…and love—

She jerked her hand back. That was not going to happen. She wasn't going to put her heart on the line. She wouldn't get hurt again, because she knew whoever she loved would eventually disappear from her life. And that was agony she couldn't live through again. She refused to put her tattered heart on the line. The price was just too steep.

And once Graham got what he came for—the residents' agreement to move out early—he'd be gone. Her apartment would be empty. And her stepmother would be right—she wasn't worthy of love.

"I've got this." Alina put a respectable distance between them.

His confused gaze searched hers. "I'd like to help. Will you let me?"

She wanted to argue the point but didn't. Instead she nodded her reluctant agreement.

This time she made sure their fingers and any other body parts didn't touch. However, as the silence stretched out, the more awkward it became. She glanced through the full branches at Graham. What had happened for him not to enjoy the holidays? She was curious about that and so much more about him.

"Tell me more about the holidays when you were young." The words came tumbling out and then she froze, wondering if she'd overstepped.

He shrugged. "I already told you."

There was something he was holding back. And by the way the muscle twitched in his jaw, it was something serious. But she couldn't drag it out of him. She had to wait until he was ready to talk about it.

They finished wrapping the tree in lights and then sat down on the couch. Graham turned to her. "What were your Christmases like?"

She smiled as the memories came flooding back to her. "They were happy. My mother loved

the holiday. She used to say she wished it was Christmas year-round."

"That's a lot of Christmas."

Alina nodded. "She used to decorate the entire apartment," she said, gesturing at the space around them.

"This apartment?"

She nodded. "You didn't know I grew up here?"

"I had no idea." He leaned forward and retrieved one of the red glass ornaments and affixed a hook to it. "Did you ever want to move away?"

"I thought about running away after my father remarried. I wanted to be anywhere but here."

"You and your stepmother never got along?"

"We did, in the beginning. But looking back now, I think it was a show to impress my father so he'd think it was all right to remarry. But once she had that ring on her finger, things change There were rules for me and extravagances for stepsisters. She claimed I was spoiled and u But I wasn't. She lied." Alina pressed her gether, realizing she shouldn't have said al

"She was jealous of you?"

"I don't know. I can deal with a lot just not lying. Why do people have

"She wasn't the only one that lie she?"

"I can't afford an apartment in the city without the rent control and I like my neighbors. They're like family. Considering I have none of my own, I need them. And I know they need me, too— especially some of the older residents who don't have family or their families have busy schedules and don't visit very often."

"You try to fill in the gaps. And that's why you don't complain when their faucets leak more than is normal."

"Something like that."

She never talked about this stuff with anyone. It was too personal, too painful. But she knew for Graham to understand the significance of the Stirling, she would have to bare her soul, no matter how much it hurt to pull back the scabs on her past.

They'd trimmed the tree.

And by the time they'd finished, it felt as though a bond had grown between them. They were no longer strangers. They were friends.

Graham found comfort in the thought of Alina being his friend. But in the next breath, he had to wonder if friendship was the right terminology. Because he'd never longed to kiss any of his friends.

There was something about being close to Alina. They didn't even have to be touching for him to feel her draw. It was like she was the sun and he'd been pulled into her orbit, soaking up the rays of her smile.

But he knew that none of this was going to last. It was all an illusion created by their temporary closeness and the magic of the holidays. Once Christmas passed, he'd be back in his sterile and cold apartment. And Alina would never want to see him after he tore down the Stirling. So it was best not to let himself get drawn in.

Graham paused to look up at the tree. In his hand he held a white, glittery glass ornament. And for the life of him, he couldn't find a spot to hang it. The tree was covered with lights, ribbon and ornaments.

He wanted to say it was overdone, maybe even gaudy, but he couldn't say any of those things. There was a method to Alina's madness and, in the end, the tree looked amazing. It sparkled and shined like fine jewelry.

And at the same time, it was filled with memories. Graham knew this because Alina had told him the history of each of the unique ornaments as she hung them on the tree. In the end, the tree was like the story of her life. No wonder she liked it so much.

He didn't have anything like that, but in the next breath, he realized that wasn't true. He had the company his father had left to him. It was filled with memories, from the first time he could remember sitting in the CEO's chair when he wasn't even big enough for his feet to touch the ground to interning when he'd been in college.

And then there was the time he'd gotten to shadow his father throughout the day. It had been bring-your-child-to-work day and he'd badgered his father until he'd agreed to take him to the office. It was that day Graham had sworn to himself that one day he would run the company just like his father had done. He just never thought that day would arrive so soon.

He also remembered his mother's reaction to the reading of the will—the part that gave Graham controlling interest in the company. His mother had begged him to sell it. He'd refused.

She'd told him that in order to successfully run the company he would have to make sacrifices. Back then he'd thought he'd had all of the answers. He told her he was man enough to make all of the sacrifices necessary. He hadn't wanted to hear a word his mother said if it was contrary to him living up to his duty as the Toliver heir.

"What do you think?" Alina's voice interrupted his thoughts.

He blinked and turned to her. "What?"

"The tree. Do you like it?"

He paused to take in the tree once more. "I think it's amazing. It's you."

"It's me?" Her fine brows scrunched together. "You think I look like a tree? A skinny top and a fat bottom—"

"No! I don't mean you as in you literally, but it's made up of little pieces from your life."

Her brows smoothed and then a smile lifted her pouty lips. "Yes, it is. I never thought of it that way. Is that the way your little Christmas tree was?"

He shook his head. "We always had the same designer ornaments that came as a set."

"What was Christmas morning like? Or were you so rich growing up that you didn't care about Santa bringing you presents?"

"I wasn't as spoiled as you might imagine. My father believed I needed to earn what I got. I don't even remember how young I was when he started saying that. For all I know, he could have said it as soon as I was out of diapers because I can't remember anything else."

"Your father sounds like a tough man."

Graham shrugged. "He had his moments of softness, like when I had pneumonia. I never saw him so worried. But once I was better, things went back to normal."

"Well, Christmas at the Stirling is all about family."

"But you're not related to these people."

"Not biologically, but they're my family by

choice. So we celebrate the holiday by having a potluck dinner and doing a Secret Santa exchange."

"That sounds nice."

"It is. It's not about the extravagance of the presents. It's about the company. And you're welcome to join us this year. That is, unless you're spending the holiday with your mother?"

"Uh, no." He shook his head. "My mother and I haven't spent the holidays together since before my father died. We...we had words." He picked up a small silver ball ornament and rolled it around in his hand. "She accused me of turning into my father."

"I take it that's not a good thing."

"Not the way she meant it. She said I was going to let the business take over my life. I told her I could balance things, but she didn't believe me."

"Is she right? Or do you have more dates than you can count?"

He arched a brow. "Why? Are you planning to ask me out?"

Her asking him out?

The idea didn't sound as preposterous as it should.

Immediately heat flamed in Alina's cheeks. "Of course not. I just wondered if your mother was right. Do you have a life outside the office?"

Graham placed the ornament back in the box. "I don't have time." He got to his feet. "Why can't anyone understand that it takes a lot of time to run a company the size of Toliver? Once I get a firm hand on everything, things will change. I'll have more time."

She knew he wanted to believe that, but she had her doubts. "My father used to say you had to pick what was important in life and then make a concerted effort to make time for what makes you happy."

He frowned at her. "So you're siding with my mother."

"I'm not. I'm just trying to understand."

"Never mind. It doesn't matter. Once this agreement is over, you'll never have to see me again." And with that he started to walk away.

"Graham, wait. That isn't what I meant."

With his back to her, he waved her off and kept walking right out the front door.

Ugh! That had gone totally wrong. She hadn't meant to upset him. She shouldn't have said anything, but she thought they'd reached a point where they could talk to each other openly, like friends. As his friend, she worried that his mother might be right.

Not that she wanted him to date her or anything. Far from it. They were too different from each other. She loved Christmas. He couldn't care less about it. He loved working at all hours. She only worked the long hours out of necessity. She craved a big, loving family. He seemed happier being alone. They definitely didn't belong together.

But that didn't mean she didn't feel bad about the way the conversation went. It was getting late, maybe they were both tired. She'd apologize to him in the morning.

Oh, who was she kidding? There was no way she'd be able to sleep with things left like this. And so she stood and headed for the door.

She pulled open the door to find Graham standing there. His head hung low as he shifted his weight from one foot to the other.

"I'm sorry," they both said in unison. And then they both smiled.

"I shouldn't have said anything," she said. "I know you're doing your best."

"And I shouldn't have let it bother me. It's true. I work a lot. But it won't be forever."

She wanted to ask if that meant he was planning to marry and settle down with a family of his own. Suddenly the image of his arm around a tall, slender woman with perfect hair filled Alina's imagination. The thought stirred unease in the pit of her stomach. Refusing to acknowledge what it might mean, she shoved aside the thought.

"Well," she said, "I'll just go clean up and call it a night."

"I'll help you."

"You don't have to—"

"I want to." His tone was firm.

"Thanks. That would be great."

She breathed easier as together they walked back to the living room. She was starting to see that this challenge of getting him to see the apartment building as something more than an obstacle to his goals was going to be more difficult than she'd originally envisioned.

How did she draw him into the charm of the building without making things personal? Because they needed to keep their distance. No matter how handsome or thoughtful she found him, they came from different worlds.

Even with that warning in mind when she glanced over at him, she felt a flutter in her chest. This was going to be so much harder than she'd ever imagined.

CHAPTER ELEVEN

HE'D NEVER BEEN so busy.

And yet Graham found himself happier than he'd ever been.

Monday morning he'd slipped away from the Stirling for a very important meeting. He was hoping to persuade a couple that owned a sizable company to go in on a project with his company, considerably lowering Toliver's financial obligation. However, when the topic of the holidays came up, he soon learned they loved Christmas celebrations.

And when they'd mentioned spending Christmas in New York, there had been a miscommunication. They thought he was inviting them to a party. What was he supposed to say to that?

He'd known that this was his chance to solidify their relationship so of course he had to invite them to his big Christmas gala. The only problem was he didn't have one planned. His company never held or sponsored holiday events. And now Graham had exactly eighteen days to plan a huge Christmas party.

He thought of handing it off to his assistant, Mary, but he just couldn't bring himself to do that to her—even though he knew she wouldn't have complained. She was a newlywed and she already had her hands full picking up some of his work while he was working from home.

He would deal with the party himself—something he'd never done in his life. He figured he'd start with the location but that was proving impossible. Venues large enough to hold such an event had been reserved a year or two in advance.

It was late in the afternoon when Alina stopped by his place. "The restaurant was busy all day and I had not one but two Christmas parties. I just came home to change my clothes before heading back." She gestured to a large red stain on her white blouse. "It was a rough day."

He stared up from where he was sitting on the floor leaning back against the wall with papers scattered around him. "You're going back so soon?"

She shrugged off her coat, then draped it over her arm. "It's fine. It'll slow down after the holidays. How was your day?"

He closed his laptop, giving her his full attention. "I'd rather hear about your day."

She studied him for a moment. "What's the matter?"

"Why would you think something's wrong?"

"Because you get those little lines between your brows when you're worried about something."

"Wait. Are you saying we've spent that much time together that you can read me?"

"Yes. Now, tell me what's wrong. Is it Merryweather? Is he giving you a hard time?"

"No. I picked him up some cookies on the way home from the office and he loved them. It has nothing to do with the building."

"That's a relief." She resisted the urge to point out the fact that he'd referred to the Stirling as his home.

He rubbed the back of his neck. "I have a problem at the office."

"Anything you want to discuss?" She sat across from him on one of his new chairs. It would be nice to focus on someone else's problems for a change.

Graham hesitated. "I have potential clients coming into the office the week of Christmas and I really need to impress them."

"You're the best at what you do and your offices are beautiful, so I'm not seeing the problem."

"It's not enough. I know a couple of other companies are courting them. So I need this visit to stand out in their mind."

"I take it we're not discussing your business presentation."

He shook his head. "That's already under control. But I sort of invited them to a Christmas party that doesn't exist."

Her mouth gaped. "How in the world did you do that?"

"I'm not exactly sure but now they're making plans to return for this impressive Christmas gala."

"Graham, do you know how close it is to Christmas? People make these plans months or a year in advance."

His frown deepened. "Now what am I supposed to do?"

"You have a nice apartment. You could throw an informal party there."

He shook his head. "They're flying in from Phoenix. They're expecting something spectacular. Not a little dinner party."

"Hmm… I see." She racked her brain for an easy solution. "I can't even offer the Christmas Café. It's booked solid."

Graham lifted both arms and raked his fingers through his hair. "What am I going to do? This account is very important."

"One of the things I ask clients before planning a party is about their likes and dislikes. Have you researched these people to find out their interests?"

He nodded. "I didn't learn much."

"There was nothing about what organizations they support?"

"Well, I did find this." He opened his laptop and started typing. It took him a moment. "Here it is."

She accepted the laptop from him and started to read. A few minutes later, she said, "This is great."

"How do you get that?"

"It says that Mrs. Cortinas is a proud sponsor of the arts."

"And…" His dark brows knitted together in confusion. "You want me to make a donation to one of her causes?"

Alina shook her head. "Let me think on it and I'll get back to you."

"On what? The party? But you said it was too late."

"I didn't say it was too late. I said most places will already be reserved. So we'll have to think of someplace less traditional. And it'll have to accommodate artwork because if the wife is impressed, she'll make sure the husband gives your presentation more attention."

"I hear you," he said. "But it's not going to work."

"But why? Are you afraid they'll learn you're a grinch?"

"I am not."

She crossed her arms and arched a brow. "Remember, I've been to your office. I know it's devoid of decorations."

"My father didn't believe in wasting the time and money on decorations when everyone was supposed to be there to work, not to have a party."

"I hope you don't mind me saying that your father was way too serious."

"How could I mind when I agree with you?"

"You do?" When he sent her a crooked smile and nodded, her heart fluttered. Refusing to let him see how he affected her, she turned her attention back to the laptop.

"I found another article that says the Cortinas decorate their home for the holidays." She followed the link he gave her. "Here. See."

He leaned over to look at the monitor. In the process, he grabbed the other chair and pulled it up next to hers. She pretended like his closeness didn't bother her as she clicked through the online photos. But her heart was pitter-pattering as her pulse raced. She had to think about something other than the way his shoulder was brushing against hers.

"Do you see all of the artwork on the walls?"

"I do. But how does knowing she likes art-work help us?"

"Those pieces aren't classic pieces of art. I'm not an expert, but I'm thinking those were all created by up-and-coming artists."

"And that helps us how?"

"I don't know yet. Let me think about it."

He sat back. "Alina, this isn't your problem. I don't expect you to fix it."

Alina glanced at the time on the monitor. "I have to go."

"Already? But you just got here. You haven't even had time to eat or rest."

"I'll be fine. It's a big event. Do you know the Hulligan Group?"

He nodded. "They're a big financial firm."

"And they rented out the entire café for a hol-iday party. I was told it was going to run late."

He reached out to her. His fingertips caressed her cheek, making her heart pound. "You look tired. You're on the go from first thing in the morning until you collapse in bed at night. There are lunch parties and evening parties on top of your regular shift. This is, what, your eighth party this week? Just quit. I'll pay you to plan my holiday party."

"No." She pulled away from his touch, angry that he'd disregard her job so quickly.

"My job might not be as important as yours but I like it and there are people counting on me. Now I have to go."

She jumped to her feet when Graham said, "Alina, wait. I'm sorry. That's not what I meant."

Her back was to him. Her mind said to just keep walking, but another voice said to let him explain himself. She turned to him and found him standing there with a frown on his face.

"I don't have a lot of experience talking with women. Not like this." He raised his gaze to meet hers. Uncertainty showed in his eyes. "The last woman I was involved with, well, I thought things were going good. We'd been together more than a year when she dumped me."

"I'm sorry. That must have come as a shock."

He nodded. "It did. When I asked her why, she said I was too focused on my work and she felt invisible. I don't want to make that mistake again. Not that we're dating or anything."

Was he trying to say he'd spoken out of actual concern for her? She didn't want to jump to conclusions. She'd done that with her stepmother and stepsisters and look how that had turned out.

Graham's gaze met hers. "I just meant I was concerned about you. If there's anything you need me to do, just say the word."

Her heart fluttered in her chest. He cared about

her. "Thanks for the offer. If I think of something, I'll let you know. For now, I need to go change."

She rushed out the door and headed for the steps. All the while her heart was pounding. Graham really cared about her.

A voice in her head said to be cautious. After all, he was the enemy, poised to take away her home. She wanted to say that was business, this is different—it's personal—but could you separate the man from the business?

While the CEO was away, the party planner could scheme.

Okay, so maybe *scheme* was too strong of a word. But this Christmas party was nearly impossible to plan. Even though Graham thought finding a location to hold the event would be the hardest part of this last-minute party, it was in fact the easiest since he owned the venue.

The Toliver conference space on the top floor of the Diamond Building was perfect for his purposes. Though Graham thought it was too cold with the black-and-white decor, she knew the right decorations could change the starkest room into a cozy Christmas setting.

The more she thought about taking on the task of planning Graham's party, the more she saw an opportunity. Not just for Graham but for herself, too. If living here in the apartment building and interacting with its residents hadn't changed Graham's mind about the pending demolition, she was going to have to work harder. And she thought she had an idea. The only question that remained was whether or not Graham would go for it.

She knew she was going out on a limb here because planning an elaborate party in just a few weeks, well, it was a crazy notion. And yet, she found herself willing to take on the challenge because she was running out of options.

First, she'd have to come up with the theme for the party. And then it came to her: the Snow Ball. Other party details would prove to be more challenging…that is, unless you lived in an apartment building full of talented people. She just hoped everyone had the time and interest in helping her. After all, it would be asking a lot of them to help Graham, of all people.

Still, what would it hurt to ask them? And that's why she'd called the residents she was closest to and asked them to meet in her apartment.

"Thank you all for coming," Alina said. "I really need your help."

Mr. Jackson glanced around. "Where's the handyman?"

Alina smiled at the CEO of Toliver Investments being called a handyman. "Graham had a meeting at the office. I told him I would handle things here while he took care of his other work."

Merryweather crossed his arms over his chest. "Is he at the office plotting to kick other people out of their homes this holiday season?"

"He's not like that." As soon as the words were out of her mouth, Alina felt as though she was having an out of body experience. Since when had she started defending Graham?

Pearl Sanders, the sweetest eighty-year-old woman, sent her a knowing smile. "I understand, dear. He is quite handsome. If only I was a few years younger, you'd have a challenge on your hands."

Challenge? There would be no challenge. Graham wasn't hers. And she didn't want him to be. Did she?

"What I want to know is why we would help someone who's kicking us out of our homes," Grace Taylor asked.

"I don't have anywhere to go," one person said.

"Neither do I."

As other residents chimed in with their discontent at helping the enemy, Alina felt caught in the middle. It was a very strange and uneasy place to find herself.

Because she was beginning to really know Graham as a man, not the high-powered CEO. He wasn't the big mean monster that people wanted to think about him. He was fun. He was caring. And he was hot. Very, very hot.

"I understand your hesitation," Alina said. "But what if in exchange Graham had his people track down affordable housing for all of us?"

"He agreed to do this?" Merryweather asked.

"Well, uh, no." Alina worried she was about to lose any chance of them agreeing to help. "But he told me how important this party is to him. I think he'll be agreeable to our term. Trust me. I'll work it out."

Mr. Jackson frowned. "I still don't like it. No matter what they find, it won't be home. Our home."

"I know." Alina's heart ached at the thought of them all being separated. "But I haven't given up hope that he'll find an alternative building site." She'd seen Graham take to the people in the building. Tearing down this building was no longer going to be a case of faceless numbers on a report.

For a moment, everyone chatted among themselves. Alina hoped they'd see it as an opportunity to win Graham over.

"What do you say?" Alina asked. "Are we going to do this?"

Though they lacked enthusiasm, they all agreed.

"Thank you." Alina smiled at the people she thought of as family. "Let's get to work."

Everyone stated their special talents. The people who claimed not to have any talents befitting a grand party were relegated to the decorating committee. Their first task was tracking down a live Christmas tree that was relatively slender but tall, something close to twenty feet. And second on their to-do list was buying an enormous amount of twinkle lights in blue for the ceiling and white to drape about the various support posts in the ballroom and the Christmas tree.

"I know the Stirling has some snowmen in storage," Alina said. "I'll pull them out and see if they're usable."

"I'm assuming you'll want music for the event," Mr. Jackson said. He played the sax professionally until he retired. Now he and his retired bandmates played local venues. When she smiled and nodded, he said, "I suppose I could see if the band is available."

She'd wanted to ask him, but she hadn't wanted to pressure him. "Thank you. Your band is amazing. I'll mark you down. Let me know if there are any problems."

Mr. Jackson nodded before adjusting his bifocals. He started to type a message on his phone.

Merryweather offered to check with the theater where he used to work and see if they could borrow some props. Someone else had connections with an art gallery and was going to see if they could track down a bunch of winter-themed pieces to decorate the walls. Piece by piece and person by person this event was coming together.

She hoped when it was all pulled together that it would live up to Graham's expectations. She knew this event had to be high end and she planned to do everything to make it so.

CHAPTER TWELVE

A DAY OFF.

Today would be Alina's day to catch up with everything that hadn't been done around the apartment building—that is, whatever Graham hadn't been able to complete. She was expecting a really long list. She knew Merryweather always had problems—lots of problems—though most of them were quite minor.

Merryweather's family didn't live in the state and so he didn't get many visitors. And now that he was retired, he stayed in his apartment most of the time. He was lonely and she couldn't blame him.

As she rushed through her Wednesday morning routine, her thoughts returned to Graham. She'd heard from some of the residents that Graham didn't appear to have a clue about the difference between a nut and a washer, but he'd persevered. More times than not, he'd called in outside help. That wasn't surprising. She had to do that, too, when a task was beyond her ability.

But what surprised her was that he stayed and observed the hired help, even asking questions. The man was certainly full of surprises. She smiled.

When she moved to the kitchen to feed Prince, her gaze strayed over to the calendar. Time was running out before everyone had to move. Her good mood dimmed, but she wasn't giving up on a Christmas miracle.

With her coffee made, she headed for the door, planning to stop in at Graham's office. She would check to see what messages the tenants had pinned to the punchboard on the outside of the door to the building manager's office. It wouldn't hurt to give Graham a helping hand.

But no sooner had she opened her apartment door when Graham appeared before her. "Hi. I was just heading out to see you."

"Look no further." He held up a pastry bag. "And I brought goodies from the Polka Dotted Bakery. Thought you might enjoy the treat after your exhausting week."

How did he know she had a soft spot for pastries? Lucky guess. Still, it did have her retreating back into the apartment. "I can't stay long. I have to see what needs done around the building."

"Nothing."

"What?"

"Nothing needs done. I'm on top of everything."

Surely she hadn't heard him right. "Everything?"

He smiled at her. "I can tell by your one-word responses that you expected me to fail miserably at this building maintenance stuff."

Even she couldn't stay on top of everything in the building. "What about Merryweather? He always has a leak or a clog or a squeak."

"All of his faucets and drains have been tightened. His bathroom is just fine. And his door hinges have all been lubricated."

Her mouth gaped. She caught herself and pressed her lips together. "That must have taken you forever."

He shrugged. "I think that was the point."

"So you noticed he's lonely."

Graham nodded. "I started taking him cookies and staying to chat. Once I started stopping by every day or so, the repair requests slowed down."

"You know, I've been thinking of getting him a rescue dog. I figured they could help each other out. The pup would get a good home. And Merryweather wouldn't be alone and he'd have a reason to leave his apartment."

"That's a good idea. I bet he'd love it. You should do it."

Alina sighed. "I can't."

"Why not?"

And then she explained her reasoning about the move and the possible restrictions on pets. "I just couldn't do it to him. I couldn't imagine him getting attached to a dog and then having to give it up."

"And it's my fault."

She didn't say a word. Now that she was getting to know Graham, he was no longer the big bad monster she'd originally imagined. She didn't want to like him, but it was difficult not to when she found out what he'd done for Merryweather. I mean, how can you dislike a man that indulges a lonely retiree and goes out of his way to get him cookies?

In an effort to change the subject, she said, "I've been giving your problem some thought."

His brows scrunched together. "What problem?"

"Impressing your prospective partners with a big splashy party."

"Oh." His brown eyes lit up. "What did you think of?"

"How about a Snow Ball?" She smiled at her pun. "Get it? Snowball as in something to make Frosty out of. And a Snow Ball as in a winter dance."

"Cute." He smiled but it didn't reach his eyes. He didn't like it. "I'm sure they'll be invited to scads of parties."

Though her excitement had been punctured,

she wasn't giving up. He hadn't heard the whole idea yet. "Perhaps, but this would be a chance to show them that you support local artists."

His eyes widened and she could tell she had his full interest. "What exactly do you have in mind?"

"I don't have any specifics but it can't be that hard to get a bunch of local artists to come together for a party. It would be free publicity for them. Who would pass that up?"

"I don't know. There isn't much time until the party. They might already have other plans."

She wanted the party to also represent some of Graham's interests. "What do you enjoy about winter? Maybe something you liked to do as a kid."

He shrugged. "When I was a kid, I'd go sledding."

"What about going to the tree lighting at Rockefeller Center?"

He shook his head. "My mother hated the noise and rush of the city."

"Oh." Alina couldn't imagine anyone not loving the energy of New York City. There was no other place she wanted to live. Ever.

"About this party," Graham said, "I just don't see being able to make it work. There's too much to do and not enough time."

"What would you say if I were to tell you I already started planning it?"

His brows rose. "You did?" When she nodded her head, he asked, "But how? This is *the* party season. Everything is going to be reserved."

He was right. If she were to pull this party off, it would have to be by nontraditional methods. But then again, when had that ever stopped her? When Mrs. Campbell's oven had died, their prior landlord refused to replace it per the lease agreement, and Mrs. Campbell didn't have the money to replace it, so Alina had taken it upon herself to locate a gently used oven. She'd bartered her services to plan the seller's birthday party for their five-year-old daughter in exchange for the oven. In the end, everyone had been happy. It wasn't the only time Alina had negotiated to make things work. This would be no different.

Desperation to save her home—and to save the homes of her beloved neighbors—drove her onward. "Let me worry about the details. What would it be worth to you to pull this off?"

His gaze met hers. She saw the doubt in his eyes but she wasn't backing down. "It'd be worth a great deal."

"Then I propose I plan your party while you seriously consider another site for your high-rise."

"There is no other site."

"You aren't even trying!"

"Don't you think we did that before we started

buying up property here? I can show you all of the paperwork, if you don't believe me."

It was worth a try. And with a heavy heart she said, "I believe you."

"I'm sorry." His deep voice sounded sincere.

She wasn't giving up. She had a backup plan. "Fine. If I do this, if I plan you a grand holiday ball, I need you to find affordable housing for all of the residents of the Stirling." Her gaze met his. "Can you do that?"

"I… I don't know."

She pointedly stared at him. She wasn't going to back down. This party was going to be the biggest and most challenging of her career.

When he looked at her, she crossed her arms, pressed her lips into a firm line and narrowed her gaze. He had to know that she meant business. She wouldn't budge from this demand.

After a moment of tense silence, Graham said, "Okay. I'll get some people at the office started on it, first thing in the morning. But I can't promise you'll like what they come up with."

"All I'm asking for are some legitimate options for people who didn't ask to have their home demolished."

"I understand. I'm just surprised you didn't ask for something for yourself."

She shook her head. "I don't need anything special."

There was a look in his eyes—was it respect? She wasn't sure. But she hadn't done anything more than someone else in her position would have done.

"Alina, you're the most giving person I know, but sometimes you have to slow down and do what's best for you."

She waved off his concern. "I'm fine. Prince and I will land on our feet. We always do."

This time there was concern in Graham's eyes. "You can't ignore your own needs forever."

If he was talking about her lack of a boyfriend, she was too busy. She'd date again. Someday.

Her stepmother's voice echoed in her mind. *"You're too chubby, Al."* She always called her Al because she knew it bothered Alina. *"Men will never notice you. What kind of woman wears overalls and carries around a toolbox? Honestly, Al, you're embarrassing."*

Right now, she didn't want to examine what was missing from her life. "We better get started on the party," she said, hoping her voice didn't betray the way he unnerved her. "We have a lot of details to go over."

And so they got to work. The more they dove into the details of the party, the more she was able to push away the disturbing memories of the past. It seemed Graham was a good distraction, in more ways than one.

CHAPTER THIRTEEN

THEY'D BEEN BURNING the candle at both ends.

Since assuming the CEO role, Graham was used to really long hours. It was nothing, though, compared to balancing his business and the needs of the Stirling residents. Even he was getting a bit burned out.

And then there was Alina's nonstop schedule. To make matters worse, Christmas was her favorite time of the year and she was missing most of it. He blamed a lot of it on himself. In his rush to please a potential business partner, he hadn't considered how much effort the party would take.

He promised himself that, going forward, he would make things easier for her—as much as he could. He'd start with a bit of fun and, after that, he'd make sure she had a warm meal waiting for her each evening when she got home from work—whatever hour that might be.

And he was going to put his plan into action today.

Alina might not believe it, but he did know how to have a good time. After all, he'd grown up in the country. He'd learned how to pass the time, even if it had been a lifetime ago. Somewhere along the way, he'd forgotten those good times. Somewhere along the way, it'd become all about proving himself to his father, which led to a distance between him and his mother.

His mind reached for those foggy memories that he'd pushed away many years ago. The faces of those childhood friends came back to him. In the winter, they were always outside when it snowed. Winter had been one of his favorite seasons. So when had it all changed? When did the fluttering snowflakes change from something exhilarating to something aggravating because it would tie up traffic even more than normal?

"Alina?" he called down the hallway. "Alina, hurry up."

It was Thursday and she'd finished working early. She was now changing out of her work clothes, but it seemed like it was taking her forever. And now that he remembered how much fun winter could be, he was anxious to share some of that fun with Alina.

"Alina—"

"Okay. Okay." She stepped into the hallway in jeans and a green sweater with a Christmas tree on the front with gold jingle bell ornaments. "What's with the rush?"

"We have things to do. Come on." Graham shrugged on his winter coat.

Alina moved toward him with a confused look on her face. "What has gotten into you? I thought you had a report to get to your board."

"It can wait. This can't."

She arched a brow as her gaze studied him. "You are acting mighty strange."

"Not strange. Mysterious. Yes, mysterious sounds a lot better."

In no time, they were bundled up and headed out the door into lightly falling snow. Graham adjusted his black knit cap. He couldn't remember the last time he'd set aside an important project to go play in the snow.

He glanced over at Alina, all bundled up in a red coat with a matching knit cap with the design of white snowflakes. There was just something about being around her that reminded him of the person he used to be many, many moons ago.

"Where are we going?" Alina asked.

"You'll soon see." He took her gloved hand in his as he led them through the maze of people crowding the sidewalk.

A quick subway ride and a short walk later they arrived at Central Park. The area was a bustle of activity. Young and old alike were out and about, enjoying the holidays.

As they made their way to the edge of the ice rink, Alina looked at him. "We're going ice skating?"

He smiled and nodded. "You wanted to know what I used to do at Christmastime."

Her gaze moved to the ice with people of all ages gliding along the ice and then her attention returned to him. "You can skate?"

"Don't look so shocked. I used to do a lot of things before I became a busy executive. When I was young, my mother would take me to a local ice rink. And when I got older, I would go skate with a friend on their pond." When he saw Alina staring at him with surprise in her eyes, he said, "You surely didn't think I was born in a three-piece suit, did you?"

"No. It's just that you're all about business 24/7. It's surprising seeing you in a different light."

With her hand still in his, he said, "Let's go rent skates." When he turned to start walking, she didn't follow. He turned back to her. "What's wrong?"

"I can't skate." When a smile lifted his lips, she said, "It's not funny."

"I'm not laughing. It's my turn to be surprised. Who'd have thought there's something you don't know how to do."

"What's that supposed to mean?"

"That you, my darling, are a jack-of-all-trades." It wasn't until he finished speaking that he realized he'd called her "my darling." Where in the world had that come from?

"When you lose a parent, you learn to help out. When you lose the other parent, you learn really fast how to provide for yourself—even if it means slinging a toolbox."

He gave her hand squeeze. "I'm sorry you lost both of your parents."

"I am, too." Her voice was so soft it was more like a whisper that floated away in the breeze.

As they stood in line to get skates, Graham said, "Don't worry. I'll teach you to skate."

"You might regret making the offer. I can just see me falling face-first and taking you down with me."

"It won't happen."

She arched a fine brow. "How can you be so sure?"

"Because I'll be there to make sure it doesn't."

Once they had their skates laced up, Graham helped Alina out onto the ice. This time she was the one reaching for his hand. She wrapped her fingers around his and squeezed like a steel vice. His fingertips started to lose sensation.

"Relax," he said.

"I can't."

"Listen to the music. It's a Christmas song. And we all know how you love the holiday classics. Maybe you could sing it."

She frowned. "What does a song have to do with me skating?"

"Because if you don't relax a little, my hand is going to lose all blood flow."

Her mouth formed an O as she eased up her hold. "Sorry."

He stretched his fingers. "All I'm saying is that you can't skate when your muscles are tense. I promise this isn't that hard."

Her eyes narrowed. "You keep saying this is easy, but I still haven't seen you skate."

"Is that a challenge?"

She eagerly nodded. "It is."

"Are you fine staying there against the wall?"

She nodded again.

"I'll be right back." He took off around the rink. Luckily it wasn't too crowded.

It'd been a while since he'd been on skates, but for him it was just like riding a bike. He took a couple of warm-up passes. Then he moved to the center of the rink where there were fewer people. He attempted a jump. He didn't have much height and his landing was a little off, but he was still impressed he was able to do that good considering how long it'd been since he'd been on skates. Next, he tried a spin and did marginally better.

Hopefully it'd be good enough to convince Alina to trust him.

He skated up to her, noticing her death grip on the wall. He smiled at her, hoping to ease her anxiety. "So what did you think?"

"I think you must have been a professional skater in another life."

His smile broadened. "Not even close. But do you now trust me to guide you around the rink?"

Her eyes held doubt, but she placed her hand in his. "Let's try it."

He moved behind her, placing his hands around her waist. "I've got you." When she let go of the wall, he said, "Keep your skates shoulder-width apart." She adjusted. "Good. Now bend your knees just a bit." When she did, he said, "Not so much. There you go. And now push off with your right leg."

When she pushed off, he let her go—let her glide on the ice by herself. But when she slowed to a stop, he was right there to lend aid. They worked together on her skating as they made their way around the ice.

He let go of her hand, picked up speed and then turned so he was skating backward. Alina smiled at him. She looked adorable with her cheeks pink from the cold.

"Are you having a good time?" he asked.

"I love this. I never knew what I was missing."

"Good. We'll have to come back."

It wasn't until he'd spoken the words that he realized he'd implied they had a future. And he knew that wasn't the case. When he bulldozed her home, any thought of them doing anything together would also be demolished. The thought saddened him because he couldn't remember the last time he'd had this much fun and it was all thanks to Alina.

"I'd like that," she said, making him feel even worse.

He shoved aside the troubling thoughts of the future. Instead he focused on the here and now. He slowed to a stop, but Alina wasn't so good with stopping. She ran into him. He absorbed the impact, keeping them standing. Her soft curves leaned into him and instantly there was a chemical reaction.

When he looked down at her, he couldn't remember what he was about to say. His gaze lowered. Her rosy lips beckoned to him.

His heart lodged in his throat. He was about to live in the moment and deal with the consequences later. He lowered his head and claimed her mouth. He wasn't sure what sort of reaction his hasty action would receive, but Alina didn't push him away. Her lips moved beneath his. And in that moment, he realized he'd never had a kiss like this one, where it warmed him from the inside out.

He knew all of the reasons this shouldn't be happening, but the pounding of his heart drowned out those reservations. There was just something so special about Alina, from her determination to her thoughtfulness. How could any man resist her charms?

As her smooth lips moved over his, he wished their circumstances were different. He wanted to follow this kiss up with another and another. Because as sure as he was standing there, he would never get enough of Alina. That was a complete and utter impossibility.

The laughter of kids nearby had him pulling back. Even though it felt as though time had stopped, their kiss had been brief—much too brief.

His gaze met hers but he couldn't read her thoughts. This had been a moment of weakness. He knew to consider it anything else would be a big mistake. In the end, he would hurt Alina when inevitably her home was replaced with Toliver Tower.

"I think we should call it quits for today," he said.

She averted her gaze. "I agree. It's been a long day."

The ramifications of his spontaneous action

were already sinking in. They skated over to the other side of the rink, where they'd left their belongings in a locker. This time he didn't hold her hand.

There had been a distinct shift in their relationship. He hadn't just tiptoed over the line of common sense, he'd barged right over it with both feet. There was no taking it back. No changing history.

And as much as he'd like to see where this relationship would lead them, he couldn't do that. To follow that kiss up with more would lead Alina to believe this was the beginning of something and that wasn't the case. As it was, their time together was quickly drawing to a close.

His phone buzzed.

The following day, Graham was in no mood to speak to anyone. All he could think about was how Alina had gone out of her way to avoid him since that kiss. And he missed her—missed their friendship.

His fingers pounded harder than necessary on his laptop keyboard. He'd been on a roll and actually making a dent in his email. Maybe if he ignored the call, they'd give up and not call back. He knew he wouldn't be that lucky. Still, he continued typing.

Graham had forwarded the calls and texts from

the Stirling to his phone. By doing this, he freed himself from having to sit in the manager's office at the apartment building. It had come in handy the day before when there had been important meetings at the office about the new building.

He checked his phone, finding whoever had rung had left him a voice mail. He listened to it and found it was from the tenant in apartment 104—Alina's stepmother. If he didn't take care of it now, he knew she'd come knocking on his door. It was best to just get it over with.

He finished an email to his assistant, closed his laptop and then grabbed his toolbox—er, Alina's toolbox—and headed out the door. The one thing he'd learned since taking on this arrangement was that he wasn't so bad at multitasking. He used to like to work on one project until it was completed, but he was finding periodic breaks gave his subconscious a chance to work out problems. When he returned to his project, he had a fresh perspective.

He stepped into the deserted hallway. It was the middle of the afternoon and most people were still at work. He made his way to 104. The door was still plain, whereas most of the doors in the building had holiday wreaths or bows affixed to them. Maybe Alina's stepmother hadn't gotten around to it yet.

He raised his hand and rapped his knuckles on the door. "Maintenance."

The door immediately swung open. A tall woman with short platinum blond hair frowned at him as though she'd been standing there waiting on his arrival. It must be something serious. He inwardly groaned because he had notes about an important contract to finish typing.

"It's about time," she snapped.

Wait. What? He'd just gotten the message a few minutes ago. "I got here as fast as I could. What's the problem?"

The woman glanced past him, into the hallway. "Where's Al… Alina?"

If she thought she was going to rattle him, she had another thought coming. "She's not available. But if you'll just show me the problem—"

"It's Alina's job!" The woman's eyes darkened with anger. "I told you this the last time you came. It's what she gets paid for. I'm not going to have one of her boyfriends—"

"I'm not her boyfriend."

The woman's eyes widened. Either the news that he wasn't Alina's boyfriend was a surprise or the woman wasn't used to anyone interrupting her when she was yelling. Either way, he didn't like the woman at all.

Suddenly her demeanor changed. A smile plumped up her drawn cheeks. "My daughters aren't here at the moment, but I know they'd love to meet you."

He didn't know where this conversation was headed, but he had an uncomfortable feeling.

"Come inside." She stepped back. "I just put on some coffee."

So much for there being an emergency. It was time to make a quick exit.

He held up a finger for the woman to wait and then he pressed on his earpiece, pretending he had an important phone call.

"Yes, Mary." He paused for a moment. "Yes, I have those numbers on my laptop. I'll get them for you. Hang on." He turned back to the woman. "Sorry, its important business."

The woman's mouth gaped as her brows gathered and her eyes revealed her utter disapproval at being dismissed.

He immediately turned and strode away. His dislike for Alina's stepmother was intense. Behind him a door slammed shut.

The funny thing was that most of the people in the building were super friendly. Others weren't as talkative, preferring to keep to themselves. But that woman was the meanest person in the building. He felt sorry for Alina—not only because she had to deal with that woman on a regular basis, but also because it was the closest Alina had to family.

CHAPTER FOURTEEN

FOUR DAYS HAD PASSED...and neither of them had said a word about the kiss.

Alina was proud of the way she'd avoided Graham. It hadn't been easy, not with him living in the same building as her. When she'd made the deal for him to live here and work here, it'd seemed like such a good idea. Now, she utterly and totally regretted it.

Because the memory of his kiss was never far from Alina's mind. She thought about it in the shower, when she was supposed to be working and when she went to bed at night. How could she let herself be drawn to the enemy?

She felt as though she'd betrayed her friends and neighbors, who were counting on her to save their homes. And she'd betrayed herself by letting her guard down with him. In the end, he'd end up disappointing her like others had done.

Even so, it didn't stop her from keeping her word about organizing the Christmas party. She spent every free moment that week working on

He appeared to have forgotten all about it. But could she?

It wasn't like she was an infatuated teenager. She could control her emotions and do what needed done. After all, they couldn't keep avoiding each other. Perhaps she should follow his lead.

"How are you with sprinkles?"

"Decorating is my thing." He got up and washed his hands. "Where are they?"

"In the cabinet next to the fridge." In the meantime, she retrieved some of the cookie dough from the fridge.

When she glanced over to make sure he'd found the sprinkles, he was stretching to reach the top shelf. His shirt had ridden up once more. She swallowed hard as she averted her gaze. This casual relationship was going to be so much harder than she thought.

"Wow. You have a lot of them. In almost every color."

Alina smiled. "I like them. They're bright and fun."

"The only thing I don't understand is that you said you weren't good in the kitchen." The plastic bottles rattled as he removed them from the cabinet. "Yet you bake."

"Maybe there are a few things I can do in the kitchen," she admitted. "I just prefer not to."

Graham's upcoming party. The Snow Ball was taking shape.

With the aid of some of the Stirling's residents as well as a handful of Graham's employees, they'd worked tirelessly to bring Alina's brainchild to life.

The conference room was a mix of fake snow, snowballs, lighted snowmen and a tall elegant tree with homemade ornaments from a local second grade class. One of the Stirling residents was a teacher and had offered to have her class help. Considering the ball was meant to feature up-and-coming artists, Alina couldn't think of anything better.

And now she wanted to do a little something for the people who had been such big helpers with this project. She'd stopped at the store and picked up some chocolates because who didn't love chocolate? She also wanted to add some Christmas cookies to each plate. She thought of buying them, but it didn't feel right. She would bake them.

Just then she heard a knock on the door. It wasn't uncommon for some of her neighbors to stop by in the evening. As the kitchen was right next to the front door, she called out to them to come in.

When she glanced up, the breath hitched in her throat. She blinked but Graham was still standing there staring back at her. How was it possible he looked even better since the last time she'd seen him in person?

"Graham, what are you doing here?" Realizing how that might sound, she tried again. "I'm sorry. What I meant to say was, is there something I can help you with?"

"I wanted to let you know that Beverly Williams has an electrical short in her kitchen. I've turned off the breaker and called in an electrician. I just wanted you to know in case you saw a stranger in the building."

Disappointment assailed her. For just a moment, she'd hoped he was there to see her. "Thanks for letting me know."

"Should I inform anyone else?"

She shook her head as she moved about the kitchen, clearing the countertop. "We may be a smaller apartment building, but people are used to service people showing up."

He nodded. "I just wanted to check."

When he didn't move to leave, Alina felt compelled to fill the awkward silence. "Is everything going okay?" She grabbed a dishcloth to wash off the countertop. "I mean, is everything okay between you and the tenants?"

"It's fine." He arched a brow. "That is unless someone complained. Have there been complaints?"

"No. None at all."

For the first time since he'd entered the apartment, she paused and really looked at him. Graham wore a pair of low-slung blue jeans. His hair was a bit mussed up, making him look so cute. As he yawned and stretched, his gray T-shirt lifted, exposing a glimpse of his washboard abs. She inwardly groaned at being so close and yet so far away. It was all she could do not to drop the baking sheet in her hands.

Before he noticed her staring, she turned her attention back to placing the baking sheet on the counter. Finding her mouth had gone dry, she swallowed hard. "I... I'm, uh, going to bake some Christmas cookies."

"For Merryweather?"

"Some for him, but most are for the people helping with the Snow Ball."

"That's a nice idea. I hope you'll have extra so I can try one."

"There should be so long as I don't burn them."

He sat down at the breakfast bar. "What can I do to help?"

She shook her head as she got out a cutting board. "Nothing. I've got it."

"Really? There's nothing I can do?"

He seemed quite intent on staying, but why? Was it possible he wanted to move past that kiss? She chanced another glance at Graham.

"Ah…so the truth comes out now," he teased. He moved to sit down on a bar stool and then placed the collection of sprinkles on the counter. He glanced up and his gaze landed on the plastic roll in her hand. "What's that?"

She cut open the plastic wrap and peeled it back. "It's cookie dough."

His brow arched. "No, it's not. It's store-bought."

"It's still cookie dough." She took a sharp knife and sliced off a sugar cookie.

"I don't know about this. This might be considered cheating." His brown eyes sparkled with merriment. "Does Merryweather know about this?"

"Oh, listen to you." A smile pulled at the corners of her mouth as her guard started to fall. "You, mister, have no room to talk."

He crossed his arms as a smile played on his lips. "What? I don't hand out fake cookies."

"They aren't fake!" *Oh, this man!* The more he got her worked up, the more he smiled. And the more he smiled, the more she fell for him. "Your cookies aren't any better than mine. I've seen the Polka Dotted Bakery boxes in the garbage."

"You did?"

She nodded.

The smile vanished from his face. "Oh, well, you keep my secret and I'll keep yours."

"It's a deal." Alina placed the last cookie on the sheet and pushed it toward him. "You start decorating this one."

He looked at the plain round circles and frowned.

"What's wrong?"

"I'm not sure how to decorate them."

"They don't have to be fancy. Just add a few sprinkles. They'll look fine but taste even better." She started to fill the second tray with cookie dough.

She could get used to this—used to spending the evening together. It was like they were a couple. As soon as the thought came to her, she halted it.

They weren't a couple. They were far from it. Weren't they? Her heart beat faster. Because then she thought of how they'd decorated the Christmas tree together. And how they'd gone ice skating together. And the kiss, oh, the kiss. Heat flamed in her cheeks. What did she call this thing between them? Because there was something. Of that she was certain.

The cookies were decorated and baked.

The kitchen was cleaned up.

Graham didn't want the evening to end. Sure, he had reports to go over, emails that needed responses and directives to send out, but for the first time ever, he had no drive to spend his evening in front of his laptop.

His gaze moved to Alina as she settled on the couch next to the Christmas tree. That's where he wanted to be, next to her, continuing to make her smile. Thoughts of work slid to the back of his mind.

He poured two glasses of cold milk and placed a few freshly baked cookies on a plate. With the excuse of sharing a snack, he moved to the living room. He sat down on the couch, leaving a modest space between them, resisting the urge to slide up next to her.

He chanced a glance at her. His gaze drifted downward to her pink lips—her very tempting mouth. Talk about your sweet treats. But he held back because Alina wasn't just anyone. He knew she'd been hurt by people in her past and he didn't want to be added to that list.

He cleared his throat. "Time to sample the baked goods."

"But those were to hand out to the residents."

"I don't think they'll mind if we eat a few." He held out a glass to her. "And I grabbed some milk."

She smiled. "Something tells me you used to have this as a bedtime snack when you were a kid."

He hadn't thought about those times in quite

a while. These days he tried to keep his focus on the future. "I did. My mother would give me cookies and milk when I couldn't sleep."

"Did that happen often? The not-sleeping part."

He sat his glass on the coffee table alongside the cookies. He leaned back on the couch, letting his thoughts roll back in time. He'd purposely blocked those memories from his thoughts.

But Alina had opened not only her home but also parts of her past to him; how could he not do the same for her? It wasn't like she knew what she was asking. How could she know when from the outside the Toliver family looked like they should have everything? But they hadn't. Far from it.

And the thing was that Graham hadn't even known how deep some of the lies had gone until long after he'd stepped in to run the family business. And now he was in so deep that he just had to keep up appearances while he realigned the business.

"When I was young my parents for the most part lived separate lives. My father was all about living in the fast lane in the city. He wanted to be around for business dinners and arrive early at the office before the other employees."

Graham had never told any of this to anyone else, including the woman he'd almost married. Maybe that should have been a warning flag to him that their relationship wasn't as strong as it needed to be to pledge forever. But they weren't discussing that right now. "My mother preferred the calm serenity of the suburbs. She said it was better for raising a child."

"Was it?" Alina asked. "I mean, did you like living outside of the city?"

"I never really thought about it, but I didn't dislike it."

"I couldn't imagine living anywhere else. It's like this city gets in your blood and you're lost without it."

"Now that I've lived here for a number of years, I understand what you mean."

"So you don't miss the quiet of the burbs?"

"Sometimes the silence just gives way to deeper thoughts."

"And what thoughts did you have?"

"That appearances can be a front for hiding secrets." He stopped there. What was he doing digging up all of this family drama? He could feel Alina's curious gaze on him. It was his fault for starting this conversation. He might as well finish it. "My parents were all about appearances. My mother prided herself on being the perfect wife and mother. My father prided himself on being a shrewd businessman. And none of that in and of itself is bad, not until you let it rule your entire life."

In that moment, he felt Alina's touch. She wrapped her soft fingers around his hand and squeezed. "I think everyone wants to show the world the image of a perfect family."

He turned to her. "But what happens when, behind the scenes, it's anything but perfect?" He turned his focus back to the blank wall in front of him. "My mother was alone with me all week. My father would come home Friday evenings. I don't know why he bothered because all he wanted was to be left alone to concentrate on the reports he'd brought home with him. And my mother was lonely and wanted his company."

"And what about you?" Alina's voice was soft. "You must have missed him terribly. I know that I loved spending time with my father, even if it included fixing a clogged pipe. Not one of my favorite tasks."

Graham shrugged. "I had my friends."

"But they couldn't replace your father."

He recalled the past—the real past—not the snippets he often referred to when asked about his youth. "I never lived up to my father's expectations."

"I'm sure you did. Maybe he just didn't know how to communicate his feelings."

Graham shook his head. "I tried to impress him with my grades in school, but all he could see was the one mark that wasn't the best. And then I participated in sports, most any sport, hoping it would be a bridge for us, but my efforts were never enough. My father said you needed to be the best or not even bother trying."

Graham glanced at her, seeing the sympathy in her blue eyes. It made him feel uncomfortable. He didn't want people's sympathy. That's why he never opened up.

"Don't," he said.

"Don't what?"

"Feel sorry for me. I'm fine. I'm better than fine. I run one of the biggest companies in the world." Though it didn't fill the hollow spot in his chest. He told himself that if he reorganized the company, overcame his father's business errors and built Toliver Tower, it was all he needed to feel fulfilled.

"But you're not fine," Alina said in a gentle voice.

He jerked away from her hold and slid over on the couch. When he turned to her, he saw the pity in her eyes and it ignited his anger. "How can you say that? You're the one who is still living in her childhood home and refusing to move out—refusing to see what the world has to offer."

No sooner were the words out of his mouth than he regretted them. What was he doing lashing out at her? He sounded just like his father when his mother told him that he worked too many hours.

Alina gasped. Pain and disappointment shimmered in her eyes.

"I'm so sorry." He moved closer to her. "I didn't mean that. I... I wasn't thinking."

When he reached out to her, she immediately recoiled. Whatever connection they'd been building, he felt as though he'd destroyed it in one outburst.

He jumped to his feet and moved to the window that looked out over quiet Holly Lane. He raked his fingers through his hair. All the while, his jaw was clenched tight. How could he hurt Alina of all people? She was the sweetest and kindest, just ask anyone in the Stirling.

"My mother was right." His voice was soft. "I am turning into my father. No wonder she doesn't bother with me."

Guilt weighed down on him. He wanted to make this up to Alina, but he had no idea how to do it. His mother had given him an ultimatum—selling the company and having a life that included her or running the company alone. His mother would never know how much that decision had cost him. And now he doubted Alina wanted him, either.

A hand touched his bicep. "It's okay."

He turned to find Alina standing there in the glow of the Christmas tree. He wanted to wipe away the sadness from her face. "You don't know how much I want to rewind time and take back my words."

"But you're right. I am stuck here. Without any true family left, I just can't imagine letting go of the Stirling and the people in it. They make me happy. They make me feel needed."

"And I have a company but no one to share it with."

Alina reached out and cupped his face in her delicate hand. "You don't have to be alone, if you don't want to be."

Wait. Had he heard her correctly? Was she saying what he thought she was saying? Every fiber of his body longed for her—to be close to her—to breathe her essence in. But first he had to know if that's what she really wanted because he just couldn't make any more mistakes where she was concerned.

His gaze searched hers. "Alina, what are you saying?"

It was then that she lifted up on her tiptoes and pressed her lips to his. Whoever said actions spoke louder than words must have been referring to this very moment. Because as her lips moved over his, he had no doubt what she'd been saying. Her lips were definitely doing all of the talking.

And he was more than happy to be on the other end of that wordless communication.

He reached out and drew her to him. Her soft curves fit perfectly to his hard planes. But now he took the lead, heating up their kiss. Her hands reached up past his shoulders, wrapping around his neck as her fingers combed through his hair.

He no longer felt alone. With Alina right here next to him, he felt as though together they could take on the world. And for the first time in his life, he knew what it was to have someone truly believe in him.

Alina didn't judge him as not good enough like his father had done. And she didn't hold things against him that he hadn't even done yet like his mother. Alina didn't pressure him to be anyone but who he was.

In this moment, he wasn't the head of a billion-dollar corporation. He wasn't the heir to a mess of accounts that had been mismanaged. And he wasn't the mean landlord that was kicking everyone out of their homes.

With Alina in his arms, he was just a man—a man that felt worthy just by being himself. He felt the weight of the world fall away. And he stopped worrying about the future or looking over his shoulder at mistakes of the past. In this moment, he just wanted to savor the here and now for this one special evening in the twinkle of the Christmas lights.

They pushed aside the coffee table and then he grabbed the blanket from the back of the couch. As he spread it out over the floor, Alina tossed down the throw pillows.

And then with the lights off except those of the Christmas tree, Alina was once again back in his arms. He claimed her lips—her full, soft lips.

Santa had come early this year. Graham wasn't sure he was worthy of such a sweet gift. He was pretty certain he wasn't. But he was totally caught up in the moment—caught up in Alina's addictive kiss.

And so he would unwrap this most special gift. He would savor this evening and the twinkle of desire in Alina's blue eyes.

CHAPTER FIFTEEN

OH, WHAT A NIGHT!

Alina woke up smiling, remembering how attentive and loving Graham had been during the night. Like a cat after a sunny nap, she stretched. She enjoyed the way her body still tingled all over.

But when she looked around, she didn't see Graham anywhere. She paused and listened for sounds of the shower. There was none. He was gone?

It was then that she checked the time. It was after eight. *After eight!* She never slept this late. But she did have a good excuse. The best excuse.

She wrapped a blanket around her from the makeshift bed on the living room floor and jumped to her feet. She'd requested the day off from working at the Christmas Café. Everyone was meeting at the Diamond Building at nine a.m. to make the final touches on the conference room.

She still couldn't believe she'd forgotten to set

her alarm, but then again she'd been utterly distracted the night before. A smile pulled at her lips. But it soon disappeared when she realized Graham had left without saying a word to her.

What did his silent departure mean? Did he regret their night together? Her heart tumbled clear down to her frosted pink shimmery painted toes.

Unshed tears pricked the backs of her eyes. She blinked them away. Whatever his reason for disappearing, she'd have to deal with it later. Right now, she had people waiting for her. And Alina wouldn't let them down.

She rushed to the kitchen and found the coffeemaker was filled with water and ready to go with a fresh pod already loaded. She hadn't left it like that. It had to have been Graham being thoughtful. A smile lifted her lips. All she had to do was close the top and press the power button. And then she saw the note from Graham.

Sorry I had to go. You were so tired I didn't want to wake you. I had an important meeting at the office with the Cortinas.

I'll see you later, G.

She smiled. Maybe it wasn't a love note, but he hadn't pulled a disappearing act. For that she was grateful.

Then realizing the lateness of the hour, she

ran down the hallway and hopped straight into the shower. It was the fastest shower she'd ever taken.

After she dressed and threw her damp hair up in a messy bun, she realized Prince wasn't yelling at her for his breakfast. In fact, he wasn't anywhere in sight. That was strange.

"Prince? Prince?" She rushed into her bedroom, looking for him.

There was no Prince in her bed or under it. She was on her way to the kitchen when she spotted Prince in the living room stretched out on the couch. Not far away was Prince's licked-clean blue bowl with white fish ringed around it. She never fed him on the couch.

She smiled and ruffled Prince's fur. "Seems like you and Graham have made up. Huh, boy?"

Prince squeaked as he stretched. Then he settled on his other side.

It looked like she wasn't needed here. It was a strange feeling, sharing her cat. She'd never done it before. But she liked that the two males in her life were getting along.

She leaned over and kissed the top of Prince's head. "Love you. I'll be home later."

But not for long. Tonight was the Snow Ball and she had every intention of dancing with Graham. In fact, her heart was set on it.

The pep was back in her step as she gathered

her thank-you gifts and then headed for the door. She'd been worried about nothing. Things between her and Graham were the best they'd ever been.

This room was amazing.

It no longer resembled a conference room.

Graham stood in the doorway, admiring the fake snow settled around a snow people family. There was even a small snow hut made out of white foam balls. He smiled. Why had he ever worried about letting Alina run with this plan? She did amazing work. She needed to start up her own party-planning service and do it full-time.

He strolled around the room, taking in all of the artwork on the walls, from snowy mountains to quaint snowy storefronts as well as some abstract pieces. It was very impressive. He needed to thank Alina. In this case, words wouldn't be enough. It needed to be more than helping the residents of the Stirling find appropriate housing. It needed to be something special just for her.

He thought of the prior night and a smile pulled at the corners of this mouth. No matter how long he lived, he'd never forget this time with Alina. The night had been more than he dared to imagine it would be—she had been more special than he deserved.

But with their agreement about to come to an end, he knew their paths in life would lead them in opposite directions. The thought immediately deflated his mood. Even though the company was headed in the right direction, he had other things that needed his immediate attention. He finally acknowledged running a company this size would always be demanding of his time, and there was no way he wanted to end up in an unhappy marriage like his parents had endured.

And no matter what had happened between them, Alina was going to look at him differently after the Stirling was gone. The thought caused an uneasiness in his chest.

But before all of that happened, they had tonight. And he wanted to show her how much their time together meant to him. He rushed to the bank of elevators. He had a meeting with the Cortinas and then he was slipping out to find Alina a memento to remember tonight—to remember him.

Things like this just didn't happen to her.

And yet Alina stood in front of her bathroom mirror in a white evening gown that she'd picked up at a secondhand shop. She didn't have the money for a fancy, new dress. It had needed a few adjustments, the torn lace mended and a stain removed. But she'd done it.

If someone didn't know about those issues, they wouldn't notice them, right? She turned in front of the mirror and assured herself the dress would do just fine. After all, it wasn't like she would stand out in a crowd.

As her anxiety rose, so did her insecurities. Words from the past came roaring back in her mind. *"Al, you have to accept that you just aren't pretty." "Al, no one will notice you."*

She pushed away the negative thoughts. It wasn't like she was going with the intent of impressing anyone—well, maybe just one person. What would Graham think of her appearance?

She glanced at the time. There was no time for a debate. If she didn't hurry, she was going to be late. And she didn't want to miss a moment of Graham's big night. She hoped it all worked out for him. She knew how much he was counting on it.

Her makeup consisted of the usual powder and mascara. But she couldn't decide about her hair. Should she wear it up? Or down? As she lifted her hair and turned to the side, her insides shivered with nerves. Maybe down would work—

Buzz-buzz.

That was probably someone with last-minute questions about the evening's events. As she continued to ponder her hair dilemma, she pressed the phone to her ear.

Before she could utter a word, she heard, "Alina, you have to come quick."

The sound of her stepmother's voice had Alina releasing her hair. "Dorian, is that you?"

"Of course it is. Now hurry." And with that the line went dead.

Alina frowned as she stared at the phone. What could be such an emergency? And it didn't escape her notice that this happened the night of the ball. Could her stepmother be low enough to want to ruin it for her? Surely nobody could be that mean.

She glanced back in the mirror at her reflection. There was no time to debate. She opted to put her long hair up in a neat and formal French twist. Once it was secure with an army of bobby pins, she gave it a light mist of hair spray.

And then Alina, knowing Graham was occupied on this big night, went to investigate what was bothering her stepmother. Hopefully, it wouldn't take long. Graham was sending cars to pick up the Stirling residents and she didn't want to miss her ride.

Knock-knock.

The door immediately flung open. Her stepmother stood there in a sparkly navy-blue dress, but it was the frown on her face that drew Alina's attention. Her stepmother made a point of taking in Alina's dress.

"Al, what are you wearing?"

Alina struggled not to roll her eyes. "You know perfectly well that everyone in the building was invited to the ball tonight."

"But not you."

"Of course I was included. I helped plan it."

Her stepmother's face creased with deep frown lines. "But you have a building to manage."

"And it will be fine for one evening. Now if that's all you wanted, I have to go finish getting ready." Alina went to turn away.

"Not so fast," Dorian said. "You have a mess to clean up."

Dread churned in Alina's empty stomach. She would not let her stepmother ruin this evening for her. She'd been looking forward to it since they'd come up with the idea. And Graham had made her promise him a dance.

"What mess?" Alina's insides knotted up.

"Mother." Juniper, Alina's oldest stepsister, rushed into the room. She wore a hot-pink dress that was short on the hemline and long in the plunging neckline. "You have to do something. I can't get ready in the bathroom."

"Your stepsister was just about to fix the problem. Go finish getting ready in your room." Then Dorian turned back to Alina. "You, come with me."

Alina didn't want to go anywhere with the

woman. She knew when Dorian felt crossed or believed Alina was getting away with something, there was a price to be paid. What did she have in store for Alina this time?

As Alina entered the living room, she noticed her youngest stepsister, Gretel, sitting on the couch in a fluorescent green dress. Her red curls were pull up with a big green bow. She glanced at Alina and scowled.

"It's in here." Dorian pointed into the bath-room.

Alina moved to the doorway and found the toilet was overflowing. She looked at her step-mother. "You couldn't have turned off the water?"

"That's not my job. It's yours." She looked at her expectantly.

Alina inwardly seethed. This woman was going to let the bathroom flood and not care about the damage it would do to her apartment. Luckily the water pressure was low as a result of the old plumbing.

Alina gathered up her long dress, keeping it from getting wet. And then she moved slowly over the floor to the shutoff valve. It took a little bit of juggling to keep her gown safe and turn the tight valve. But at last the water was off. The crisis had been averted. And her dress had been saved. She could still make it to the ball.

She turned for the doorway. If her stepmother

thought she was going to stay and clear up this mess, she had another thought coming. When Alina looked at the doorway to tell her stepmother just that, she found the woman had disappeared. It was quite fine by Alina. The less she saw of the woman, the happier she was.

Alina had just stepped into the hallway and turned for the living room when she bumped into someone. The next thing she knew hot liquid hit her chest. The liquid seeped down to her abdomen. Alina glanced down. A coffee stain spread from her chest down over her stomach and flowed onto her skirt.

"My dress!" Tears stung the backs of her eyes.

Alina blinked repeatedly. No way would she let these people see how upset she was over her dress. Her pretty dress. The dress that she'd searched for days to find. The dress she'd dipped into her savings to buy. The dress she'd worked so hard to make presentable. The dress she was going to wear to the ball where she'd hoped to dance with Graham.

Juniper sneered at her. "Look what you did. You spilled my drink."

"You're a jerk!" The emotionally charged words clogged in her throat. Alina pushed past her. If she didn't get out of that apartment immediately, she would lose control of her emotions. And then her stepmother and stepsisters would get what they wanted, to see Alina upset. She simply wouldn't give them the satisfaction. They'd already cost her enough emotional harm.

In the background, she heard Dorian calling out to her, insisting that Alina finish her work. But Alina kept her shoulders straight and her head held high as she walked through the doorway and turned toward the stairs. With all of the anger bubbling in her veins, she had plenty of energy to burn off.

CHAPTER SIXTEEN

IT WAS RUINED.

Alina didn't need a mirror to know the extent of the damage to her dress. She also didn't need an admission from her stepmother or stepsister to know that they'd done all of this intentionally. They just couldn't stand for her to have a little bit of happiness. They had to ruin it.

This evening had meant so much to her. Someone like her didn't get invited to big, splashy parties. She was the person in the background seeing to all of the details and helping to clean up when it was over. But at last she wasn't going to be ugly, chubby Alina carrying around her toolbox. But in a blink, the opportunity slipped through her fingers.

She'd just reached her floor and yanked open the door when she ran into Merryweather. At first, he smiled at her but then his gaze moved to her dress. His eyes widened.

"Alina, what happened?"

"My stepmother and stepsisters."

"But the ball. It's time to go. I came up to escort you. The cars are waiting."

The prickling of tears started again. She glanced away from his concerned gaze and continued walking toward her apartment. "I'm not going."

"What? But you have to. You planned this whole night. Without you, none of us would get to go."

She knew Merryweather was sweet, but right now she just wanted to be alone in her misery. "You'll have to go without me. I…" Her voice crackled with emotion. She glanced down at her stained white cloth heels. A tear splashed onto her cheek. She swiped it away. "Please, just go without me."

Merryweather quietly followed her back to her apartment. All the while he muttered, "This isn't right. This just isn't right."

At her door, Alina paused and turned to him. "It's okay. I'll be fine. You should go. Enjoy yourself."

A determined look came over him. "Not without you."

"But I can't go like this."

"You aren't the only one with contacts. Go grab your stuff while I make a couple of phone calls."

She'd never seen this determined side of Merryweather. She had no idea what had come over him. There was no way he was going to fix this. She glanced down at the brown stain on her dress. It was completely ruined.

But she wasn't sure she should argue with him. This was the most animated she'd ever seen the man. Maybe it would be good to indulge him just a little. She would ride with him to the Diamond Building so he didn't have to go alone. But she wasn't getting out of the car—not like this. And then she'd come and wallow in a heaping of self-pity.

She went into her apartment and grabbed her coat and purse. She turned off the lights, locked the door and then joined Merryweather in the hallway.

When they stepped outside the building, it was snowing. And the cars that Graham had sent were gone. Alina felt bad because she didn't want Merryweather to miss the ball. He'd worked hard to help pull the event together. It was like his being involved in the planning had brought back his zest for life.

"I'm sorry I caused you to miss your ride to the ball," Alina said, wondering if she could get a taxi to take him to the ball in time.

"You didn't cause anything, my dear. Our ride will be along shortly."

Had he called for a taxi while she was in her

apartment? He must have. "Merryweather, I know you want to fix things but I'll be fine staying home." She was deeply disappointed, but that was her problem, not his. "But if you could go and make sure there aren't any problems with the party, I'd be eternally grateful."

"I'll make sure the party runs smoothly. But you're going, right? It's your night to shine."

"I don't think so. Not dressed like this." She wouldn't do anything to embarrass Graham.

Just then a Rolls-Royce pulled to the curb. The unblemished white paint and polished chrome gleamed. But what was it doing here?

"Our ride has arrived." Merryweather gestured to the car.

"What?" Alina was utterly confused. How could Merryweather, with his secondhand furniture and worn clothes, afford to hire a prestigious car like this? "You hired us a car?"

"In a matter of speaking. Now we have to hurry."

"But I can't go to the ball like this." She gazed down at the stain that was beginning to dry.

"I have a plan. Trust me." He winked at her.

And for a moment, she'd swear his eyes twinkled. What did she have to lose at this point? When he realized the stain was never going to come out of this delicate fabric, she would find her way home.

The driver, in full uniform including a black hat, opened the back door for her. She got in and slid across the seat. Merryweather climbed in next to her. And off they went. She noticed how Merryweather never gave any directions or an address.

The next thing she knew, they were pulling up to the back door of a theater—the same theater where Merryweather had worked.

"What are we doing here?" Alina asked.

"You'll soon see, my dear. Come. We don't have time to waste."

And so she followed him through the back door. Lights were dimmed and voices could be heard. There was a performance going on. As Alina listened to the voices, she recognized the lines to *Scrooge: The Musical.*

Merryweather stopped outside a dressing room. A woman approached them. She wore a friendly smile. "I'll definitely have something to fit her. I've also asked Heather to do her hair and Veronica volunteered to do her makeup."

"Perfect," Merryweather said. "But remember, we have to hurry."

"Then we best get to work."

Alina was ushered into the room. And then things moved in a flurry of activity. She tried to tell them that she couldn't pay them much but they dismissed her. They said they wouldn't accept a dime from her.

Dresses were held up to her. Brows scrunched up. There were hems and haws. And then one by one each dress was dismissed. It thoroughly confused Alina because each and every dress was absolutely stunning. But for whatever reason, these women didn't think they were fitting.

"I know," the older woman said. "I have the perfect dress. But first, we have to get her ready."

Alina's hair was brushed out and redone. Her face was cleaned off and repainted. The women talked among themselves and told her not to worry, they knew what they were doing.

With her hair done in barrel rolls held in place with sparkly pins and her face made up in neutral shades that shimmered in the light, she almost didn't recognize herself. They helped her out of her stained gown. All it was good for now was the garbage bin.

And then the older woman walked back into the room with a gown in a white protective cover.

Alina would be lying if she said she wasn't anxious to see the chosen gown.

Once the dress was hung on a high hook and the zipper was undone, the protective covering was pulled back to reveal the most magnificent light blue gown. Alina's mouth gaped. Her gaze took in the spaghetti straps that led to a plunging

V-neckline, and a fitted bodice, the tiny crystals sewn to the gown twinkling in the light.

The upper back was bare. The lower back was fitted and would hug her body. And the lower portion had a short train of light blue tulle with sparkles. Alina was speechless. They surely didn't mean for her to wear that. It was much too fancy for her.

The remaining piece was a sheer shawl that looked as if it was spun of the finest silk. Though it lacked crystals, it still shimmered. Altogether, it was quite a showstopper.

"It's so beautiful."

"Almost as beautiful as you," the older woman said. "Now hurry. We don't have much time."

"But I… I can't wear something this fancy." All she could think was if she spilled something on it she'd be horrified, not to mention working for the next year—no, make it two years—to pay for it.

"Don't be silly. This gown was made for you. Now hurry."

For a moment, Alina wondered if she'd meant the gown was literally made for her. But that was totally impossible. They didn't even know she'd be showing up until just moments ago. The woman must mean the dress would be flattering on her.

She stepped into the new gown. The women

all said it brought out the blue of her eyes. Alina never believed they would have a dress that would fit her, but this dress accentuated her bust, drew in her waist, and the hemline…well, it touched the floor because she was in her bare feet. Surely no one would notice if she were to wear her stained heels, would they?

But before she could retrieve them from next to the makeup chair, Veronica brought over a pair of azure blue heels with rhinestones. They were gorgeous. And they looked so delicate.

"I couldn't possibly wear those," Alina said, still unable to take her gaze off them. "They probably won't fit."

"But you must. They match the gown." Heather knelt down to help her put them on.

Seriously, the chances they'd fit were zip, zilch, zero. But what would it hurt to try them on? They were so pretty. The most beautiful shoes Alina had ever seen. And they definitely cost more than her month's pay and then some.

And yet as Heather slipped the shoes on Alina's feet, they fit perfectly. How could that be? Tears of happiness blurred Alina's vision. How was all of this possible?

"Oh, no. You can't cry now," the older woman said. "You'll ruin everything. And Merryweather is waiting just on the other side of that door to whisk you off to the ball."

"But how can I ever thank you all?" Alina was so touched by the acts of generosity toward her—a perfect stranger.

The older woman smiled. "It's our Christmas present to you."

"Now go. Hurry." Veronica waved her off.

"Yes, go. And have a marvelous time," Heather said.

Alina hugged each of them before heading for the door. When she swung it open, Merryweather was waiting in the hallway. Her mouth gaped as she took in his transformation. It was as though he was ten years younger and he was now done up in a fine black suit and tie. He looked quite dapper.

"Merryweather, you look downright handsome."

He blushed. "Well, I couldn't escort the prettiest belle to the ball in my old suit." He held out his arm to her. "Shall we go?"

She placed her hand in the crook of his arm. "How will I ever repay you?"

"There's nothing to repay. It is I who owes you. You've always been there for me when I was lonely and when I was being contrary. You could have given up on me, but you didn't. Instead you brought me fresh-baked cookies."

"I… I didn't know it meant that much."

"It meant the world. Now there's one thing you

should know about all of this. You have to be back at the theater by midnight. That is when the guard locks up for the night and the dress must be here by then."

Her heart swelled with love. She stopped walking and turned to him. Happy tears blurred her vision. She blinked them away. And then she leaned forward and pressed a feathery kiss to his freshly shaven cheek. When she pulled back, she said, "Thank you."

Where was she?

That's all that kept going through Graham's mind as the Snow Ball commenced. This was Alina's brainchild. Without her, none of this would have been possible.

He'd put off greeting his guests and officially kicking off the party for as long as possible. He checked the time. It was five minutes past seven and the room was crowded. He couldn't delay any longer.

Graham made his way to the stage. He stepped up to the microphone and waited as silence swept over the room. All the while he searched for Alina's beautiful face, but she was nowhere to be found.

He cleared his throat. "Thank you all for coming. First, I want to wish you all a merry Christmas. And I want to thank the residents of the Stirling because if it wasn't for them, we wouldn't be here at this wonderful party. I pride myself on setting business goals and surpassing them, but when it came to planning a holiday party, well, I must say that I dropped the ball. And the residents of the Stirling quite literally came to my rescue. Thank you each and every one of you."

And then his gaze spotted Alina standing at the back of the room. The breath caught in his throat. He forgot that he was giving a speech. All he could think was *Wow!* His gaze took in her striking beauty from her golden curls to the figure-hugging sky-blue dress that shimmered like it was covered in jewels.

Suddenly he didn't care that she was late or that he'd been worried about what might have happened to her. Right then all he wanted to do was to drink in her beauty. She was magnificent. As his gaze rose, he noticed the small smile pulling at her lips. When his gaze once again met hers, there was amusement in her eyes.

He wanted to go to her, but he suddenly recalled that he was still standing on the stage and people were looking at him expectantly to finish his speech.

He swallowed hard. "Please give a hand to Alina Martin and the wonderful people of the Stirling."

Graham stepped back from the microphone to lead a rousing round of applause. Cheers rose as the joyous sound of appreciation reverberated throughout the room.

He stepped back to the mic and signaled for everyone to quiet down. "There's some amazing food in the back. Please help yourself because if you don't, I might eat it all. No, I *will* eat it all. It's so good." Laughter filled the room. "And make sure you dance. You know, it'll help make room for more of that delicious food." There was more laughter. "Again, I hope you all have a very merry Christmas."

He turned to the band and Mr. Jackson beamed as he nodded, and then with his saxophone in hand, he turned back to his band and signaled for them to start playing "White Christmas."

As the piano started to play, Graham exited the stage. He made a beeline for the back of the room—for the spot where he last saw Alina—but when he got there, she was gone. But that couldn't be right. He turned in a circle, his gaze searching the crowd.

And then he spotted her. She was surrounded by a group of his associates—his male associates. Intense discomfort came over him as he watched her smile and chat with the men. It took him a second to identify the feeling. It was jealousy—something he'd never experienced where a woman was concerned. But it was most definitely the green-eyed monster.

"You aren't just going to stand here and let one of them get the first dance, are you?"

Graham glanced over to find Merryweather standing next to him, dressed in a black suit and white dress shirt. He didn't look anything like the man that had Graham fixing nonexistent leaks and had used a cane to get around. Tonight, there was no cane and the man looked fit as a fiddle. How was that possible?

Graham turned his attention back to Alina as she laughed at something one of the men had leaned in close to say. Graham's body tensed.

His instinct was to march over there and sweep Alina away from all of them, but did he have the right to do that? Because when it came down to it, he still had a job to do. And Alina wasn't going to be happy with what his engineers and inspectors had uncovered about the Stirling.

Merryweather said, "Graham, don't let tomorrow ruin tonight. Sometimes dreams really do happen."

"I… I don't know." All the while Graham couldn't take his gaze off Alina.

"She didn't get all fancied up for those men. You're the one she talked about on the way over here. You're the one she wanted to impress."

"She's certainly done that."

"Then why are you standing here talking to me instead of her?"

Merryweather had a good point. Why bother with the possibilities of tomorrow when there was tonight to live?

With that thought in mind, Graham headed for Alina. He bypassed people wanting to speak with him, putting them off until later. And then, at last, he was standing in front of her. His group of associates parted.

"Graham, the party is wonderful." Alina smiled at him, causing a warm fuzzy feeling in his chest. He was certain there was a name for that feeling, too, but he didn't want to delve too deeply into his feelings. Right now, he just wanted to live in the moment.

"You are absolutely breathtaking." He couldn't take his gaze off her. "But you're missing one thing."

"I am?"

He smiled as he withdrew a small velvet box from his pocket. "Here."

When her gaze zeroed in on the box, her eyes widened. "Graham, what have you done?"

"It's just a little something that made me think of you." He held it closer to her. "Go ahead and take it. I promise it won't bite."

He just hoped she'd like it. The salesclerk in

the jewelry store assured him that any woman would love it. He hoped she was right.

Alina accepted the box and opened it. She gasped as she stared at the necklace. "It's beautiful." Then she closed the box and tried to hand it back to him. "I can't accept this. It's too extravagant."

He moved his hands behind his back. "But you have to take it. There's a no-return policy."

"I'm sure the jeweler will make an exception."

He shook his head. "I mean, I have a no-return policy. I really want you to have it."

Her eyes shimmered. She blinked repeatedly. Then she once again opened the box. "It's so beautiful." She ran her finger over the diamond-encrusted snowball suspended on a white-gold box chain. "I'll never forget this night."

"Let me help you put it on."

She carefully took it out of the box and handed it to him. And then she turned her back to him. She swept her long golden curls off to the side. It took him a few tries but at last he had it fastened.

When she turned around, he said, "Beautiful."

"It certainly is."

"No." His gaze met hers. "I meant you."

Her cheeks pinkened. "Thank you."

"May I have this dance?" he asked, wanting a chance to talk to her without a rapt audience.

"I'd like that."

There was an audible groan from the men as they turned and moved off. A smile lifted Graham's lips. He got the girl—the most beautiful girl in the room. Lucky for him, it was a slower song and he was able to hold her in his arms as they made their way around the dance floor.

"Thank you," he said.

She arched a fine brow. "For dancing with you?"

His smile broadened. "Well, that, too. But I meant for tonight. This entire event was your vision. You really pulled it off. Everyone is impressed."

She glanced around, taking in the smiling people. "They do seem to be enjoying themselves. But I can't take any credit. It took a village to create this evening."

"And I owe you all a debt of gratitude."

"Does that mean you'll reconsider tearing down the apartment building?" Hope shone in her eyes.

"I've given it a lot of thought, but now isn't the time to discuss it."

The sparkle in her eyes disappeared in a blink. "You're right. I'm sorry."

"There's no reason to be sorry. I know how much the building and its residents mean to you."

They continued moving around the dance floor. He loved holding her close.

His gaze met hers and it was as though the world moved slightly off its axis. He couldn't quite explain what had happened in that moment, but he knew nothing in his life would ever be the same. He also realized that imagining anything more than this moment was a fool's errand. But it didn't keep him from hoping there would be some sort of Christmas miracle.

CHAPTER SEVENTEEN

SHE FELT LIKE a princess.

And Graham was her prince.

His hand felt natural pressed to the small of her back. Her hand fit within his other hand. It was though they were dancing among the clouds. She never even felt her feet touch the floor.

If this was a dream, she never wanted it to end. His warm smile made her heart trip over itself. How did she get so lucky to be here with him?

And to think she'd almost missed out on it all if it hadn't been for Merryweather. She still had questions for her dear friend. She wanted to know how he made all of this possible. But those questions would have to wait until later.

When she glanced over his shoulder, she noticed they were the only ones now dancing. What in the world? But the music continued to play and they continued to move to the beat.

Their audience had formed a circle. And then she caught sight of her stepmother. If looks could kill, Alina would be nothing more than a little sooty spot on the floor. On each side of Dorian were Alina's stepsisters, who looked as though they'd each sucked on a lemon. She never understood how people could live their lives being so nasty.

But tonight, nothing could ruin her good mood. Nothing at all. She was on cloud nine and she had no interest in coming back to earth. Tomorrow would come soon enough.

She leaned closer to Graham. "We have an audience."

He glanced up. "So we do."

"Maybe we should stop. I don't feel right taking up the whole dance floor."

"I agree about stopping, but how about we give them something to look at first..." Graham stopped dancing but he kept his arms around her.

What is he doing? Her heart pounded.

He bent his head and captured her lips with his own. Her breath hitched in her throat.

Oh, I know exactly what he's doing.

Suddenly it didn't matter who was watching, she was quite content right here in his strong, capable arms. His kiss was light and tender, but oh so stirring.

And she knew she shouldn't let herself fall for him. But it was too late. She'd fallen hard. It was as though they were fated to meet and she couldn't imagine her life without him in it.

When the music stopped, Graham stepped back. He lowered his arms and she immediately missed the warmth of his touch. She didn't want to let him go so soon.

But it was as if the spell had been lifted and she glanced around at all of the curious onlookers. Some people had their phones held up as though they'd been filming them. Others whispered back and forth. What in the world had gotten into them to put on such a public display of affection? Heat swirled in her chest and rushed up her neck, setting her cheeks ablaze.

Once they'd moved to the side of the room, Alina fanned herself. Her face felt sunburned, as though she'd been lying on a sun-drenched beach for hours.

"Come on." Graham reached for her hand. "Let's get a little air."

Alina had no idea where they were going, but some cool air and privacy sounded perfect. They walked to the far side of the ballroom and that's when Alina remembered about the overlook.

Graham pushed open the door and they stepped out. A glance around assured her that, at last, they were alone. For the party, Graham had set up portable heaters out here, making it comfortable.

They moved to the edge. With the evening sky for a backdrop, the Manhattan skyline twinkled with lights. It was like a stunning piece of art, only better.

"This is so beautiful," she said.

"Yes, you are." Graham's voice was deep and throaty, making her pulse race.

She turned to him, finding him smiling at her. "Shouldn't you be inside with your guests?"

"But I like it so much better out here with you."

He was saying all of the right things to make her heart go pitter-patter. "I hope the evening is meeting all of your expectations."

"It most definitely is." Desire burned in his eyes.

She swallowed hard as she tried to keep her train of thought. "I was talking about the party. You know, so you can sway your business associates to join you in that new venture."

He continued to stare at her, making her heart beat erratically. "But I'd rather talk about you and me."

She smiled and shook her head. "You're impossible."

"Am I? I guess you'll have to do something about it." He reached for her, drawing her near.

Her gaze moved to the glass door that led straight to the party. Anyone could see them standing out here. "Graham, don't you think we put on enough of a show for one night?"

The smile fell from his face. "I suppose you're right." He released her. "You wouldn't want to skip the party, would you?"

"Graham, you can't leave early after all of the hard work everyone put into this event."

"You're right, again." He sighed and turned back to gaze out over the city.

"Your business associates are having a good time, aren't they?" She'd yet to meet the people, but she hoped they approved of all the hard work to put together the party.

"They were at the office most of the day. I gave them a preview of the Snow Ball. They loved it. And we closed the deal. It was more than I ever could have hoped for—in fact, it's the biggest deal in the history of Toliver."

"Graham, that's wonderful!" This time she was the one who moved in close. When she went to place a kiss on his cheek, he turned his head. Her kiss landed smack-dab on his mouth.

It was with the greatest regret and effort that she quickly withdrew. She arched a brow at him. "You cheat."

"I like to think of it as not wasting a precious moment."

"Uh-huh."

"Anyway, after the papers were signed, they said they had to leave early. There's a snowstorm moving in and they didn't want to get stuck here for the holidays. So you have nothing to worry about. Everything worked out. And I thank you for all of your hard work."

"It's a shame they missed the ball," Alina said. "It really is special." It wasn't the dance she was thinking of as she stared deep into his eyes. This whole evening was like something straight out of a fairytale.

Graham reached out swiping a flyaway strand of hair from her face and tucking it behind her ear. She instinctively leaned into his touch.

He lowered his head, pressing his lips to hers. This time his kiss was full of raw desire. She met his touch with a roaring need of her own.

She never wanted this night to end, but sadly she only had until midnight. So she best make the most of the time she had left—

Someone cleared their throat. "Excuse me, Mr. Toliver."

Graham pulled back slightly, resting his forehead against hers. "I'm sorry for the interruption. It's my assistant. It'll only take a moment."

"It's okay." Disappointment assailed her. "Do what you need to do."

Graham straightened. He drew in a deep breath and blew it out, as though subduing his irritation at the ill-timed interruption. He moved toward the doorway where a woman was waiting for him. "Yes. What is it?"

"The members of the board have arrived."

Alina watched Graham's facial expression change from one of utter irritation to one of curiosity. She could only surmise the board's appearance was a surprise for him—hopefully a good one.

He turned back to her. Regret was in his eyes. "I'm sorry. This is important. Would you mind if we picked this up later?"

"Not at all. I have some people I need to speak to." She thought of all the Stirling residents that helped make this evening possible.

"Make sure you save me a dance. Make that a few dances."

Heat warmed her cheeks. "You've got it."

He hesitated as though he were thinking of kissing her goodbye, but then he thought better of it. He turned to leave with his assistant. And with him went any answers to her unspoken question about what was happening between them. Because there was something happening, right?

And did that mean he'd changed his mind about tearing down the Stirling? Hope took flight in her heart. Before tonight, she would have said it was too much to hope for. However, this evening had shown her that magic could happen, even in the most dire circumstances.

There had to be a way for Graham to have

his impressive tower and her to keep her home and family. She was more certain now than ever before.

The evening was flying by.

And it couldn't have gone any better.

Graham had impressed the board, not only with the new partners that would alleviate some of their financial obligations but also with this party that every board member thought should be an annual event. He fully agreed, which in and of itself was startling. Alina had brought some Christmas joy to his heart.

But his board was continuing to press him about the new tower—the one that he'd said he could start ahead of schedule. And that would mean breaking Alina's heart.

His gaze strayed to where she was speaking with her friend from the Christmas Café. They were smiling and laughing as they held flutes of champagne. He'd never seen her look so happy.

And that's why he refused to say anything about the dismal findings about the Stirling. He didn't want to tell her that the whole building needed to be replaced, whether by his high-rise or by another apartment building. In its current condition, it just wasn't safe.

But for tonight, he would keep that news from her. If she were to find out, her brilliant smile that lit up the entire room would disappear. It would be like the life had been snuffed out of the party.

Who was he kidding? It wasn't the party he was worried about, it was himself. He knew once Alina heard the news—that her home was going to be destroyed—that she would never forgive him. Could he blame her? Not really. He'd probably take the news a lot worse than her if the situation was reversed.

The hour was growing late when Alina's stepmother approached him with questions about the bonus for moving out early. This was not a conversation he wanted to have here in a crowd where anyone could overhear what was being said. And it was not a subject he wanted to get into tonight.

"This is not the place to talk about business," he said.

The woman's gaze narrowed as her shrill voice rose. "If you're trying to worm your way out of this deal, you can forget it. I have my attorney on speed dial—"

"Stop." He tried to rein in his anger. This woman was nothing but rude and mean, especially to her own stepdaughter. The fact she and her daughters were even at the ball was a mistake—a big mistake—but there was nothing he could do about it now.

Anger flared in the woman's eyes. "If Alina

convinced you to renege on our agreement, you are mistaken. So what if her dress got ruined. It was an accident. I see that she got another one."

"You ruined her dress?" He was astonished that someone could be so mean and petty.

"What are you getting so high and mighty for? I told you she got another one."

"You need to stay away from her—"

"She's the building manager, even if you're playing the part for now. We both know that isn't going to last. And when you get tired of my whiny stepdaughter, one of my daughters would be a much better match for you."

He swallowed the bile that rose in his throat. The thought of having anything to do with this woman or her daughters was nauseating. He needed them to go away—far away from Alina, where they could no longer hurt her.

He had an idea. It was an idea he'd toyed with before but always hesitated about acting on. He didn't believe anyone should be rewarded for bad behavior, especially not this woman and her two daughters, who both had their arms crossed as they stood behind their mother wearing the same evil scowls.

But there was another way to look at what he was about to do—a view from Alina's side of things. Getting rid of this woman with her angry tone and nasty comments would make Alina's world so much better. Alina wouldn't ever again have to wonder if she'd have to deal with her stepmother that day or her sniping stepsisters. And for that reason and that reason only, he was willing to make a concession.

"If you're willing to be moved out by the end of the weekend, I'll double your bonus."

Immediately the woman's face lit up but just as quickly her narrowed gaze returned. "What's the trick?"

"There's no trick. I just want you gone."

The woman's dark gaze narrowed. "Are you offering this to everyone?"

"No. This is a one-time offer."

"But the building is still being torn down, right?"

"Yes."

Gasp!

Graham's jaw clenched as he turned, hoping it wasn't Alina standing there. His hopes were dashed. Alina's face was ashen. But instead of the anger he'd expected to see on her face, there was disappointment in her eyes. And he knew that disappointment was directed right at him. He'd let her down.

If only her stepmother hadn't gotten him so angry, he'd have kept his cool. He'd have followed his plan to speak with Alina first about the dire circumstances with the building.

But now, his plan was out the window. He had to think fast. But all he could think about was how devastated Alina looked and it was all his fault. Would she ever forgive him?

CHAPTER EIGHTEEN

THE BUILDING IS being torn down. It's really going to happen.

Alina's heart sank right down to her fancy high heels. Even the thought of the designer shoes couldn't lift her spirits. Everything she thought she'd accomplished by convincing Graham that the building was so much more than a nondescript apartment building had been a lie.

He'd just been putting in his time to fulfill their agreement—an agreement that was at its end. And he didn't even have the decency to tell her the bad news first. What in the world?

She wanted to ask him, really she did. But at that moment, her mind was in complete disconnect with her mouth. She opened her mouth but no words came out. She promptly pressed her lips together.

Sally, her manager from the café, moved to her side. "You said to remind you when it was almost midnight. It's a quarter till."

Alina was still staring at Graham as though

in a trance and not the good kind—this was the kind where you are stunned because someone you cared about did something utterly astonishing and oh so hurtful.

"Alina?" Sally asked. "Did you hear me?"

She nodded.

And then with what was left of her pride, Alina straightened her shoulders, turned and headed for the door as fast as her legs could carry her. Tears pricked the backs of her eyes but she blinked them away.

In the background, she heard Graham call out her name. She didn't stop. She couldn't stop. She was a moment away from losing control. And she would not let him see her cry. No way.

As she exited the ballroom, she heard someone call out to Graham. Good. Maybe he would get distracted. Because she had nothing to say to him. The fairytale had come to a disastrous ending.

The elevator ride was slow and agonizing. When at last she made it to the ground floor, she rushed for the exit. She burst through the outer doors and into the night air. She didn't notice the fluttering snowflakes or the plummeting temperature. She started down the first set of steps toward the road, hoping a taxi would come to her aid. But she didn't see any in sight. How could that be? This was Manhattan, after all. There would be one shortly. There had to be.

"Alina, wait!" Graham's voice carried through the evening air.

He hadn't waited to tell her the news about the building first, so she didn't feel any compulsion to wait for him now. Her vision blurred with unshed tears. She kept moving. And then the Rolls-Royce pulled up to the curb. How was this possible? It's as though he'd been waiting for her.

She'd just reached the car when a sudden gust of wind swept over her. It chilled her to the bone and the strong air current swept off her shawl. She turned to see it flutter in the air and float away.

There was no way to catch it while avoiding Graham. She hopped in the car. "Please go."

The car immediately pulled out. She leaned her head back against the leather seat. What had she been thinking all of this time? Like there was something serious going on between her and Graham? For him it was all business. She was the only one letting her heart get in the way.

How had such a perfect night gone so terribly wrong?

The next morning, a vision of Alina at the beginning of the ball filled Graham's mind. It was quickly replaced with the devastated look on her face when she'd heard him say he was tearing down her home. He groaned in frustration.

He hadn't slept all night. After Alina had driven off, he'd caught a taxi and gone immediately to her apartment. When she wasn't there, he figured she'd gone to a friend's place and he'd have to try and speak to her tomorrow instead.

He hadn't wanted to, but he'd gone back to the party to make sure it was shut down properly. He knew it was just an excuse not to go to his apartment alone. Because he knew when he did, he'd never get any sleep.

Graham glanced down at the shimmery wrap that Alina had lost when she'd left the ball. He'd thought for sure the gust of wind would have swept it halfway across the city, but instead the wind stopped when the wrap reached him and, as if planned, it'd landed in his hands.

He wrapped it around his hands and unwrapped it as he tried to decide the best form of damage control. He was good at it when it came to the business, but when it came to his personal life, well, that was another story.

He'd never been successful at personal relationships because he'd never been invested. But things were different with Alina. She was different. And he was different when he was with her—for the better, he liked to think.

He lifted the wrap and inhaled. A jasmine scent clung to the delicate material. He inhaled deeper and smiled. He knew as long as he lived that he'd never smell jasmine again without thinking of her.

But he wasn't a man to give up without a fight. Sure, she'd been shocked last night when she'd heard the news, but after some sleep, maybe she'd see things in a new light.

And so he took a quick shower and dressed. With damp hair, he rushed out the door. He didn't care that it'd snowed overnight and there were a few inches on the ground. Or that below those few inches was ice.

He pulled out from his underground parking spot and set off for Alina's apartment. Not all of the roads were plowed, especially the side roads, so it was slow-going. If he hadn't been in such a rush, he'd have realized that public transportation would have been far faster. But he wasn't exactly thinking clearly.

When he finally made it to the Stirling, he rushed up the stairs to Alina's floor. He hoped she was there. With rapid strides, he approached her door. He knocked. When the door didn't immediately open, he knocked again.

"Alina, please open up. We need to talk."

"Graham, go away. There's nothing to say."

He wasn't a quitter. "Not until you hear me out. I'm going to keep standing here and keep yelling through your door until you give me five minutes." When she still didn't open the door, he said, "And I brought back the wrap you lost last night."

The lock clicked and then the door opened. Alina stood there in her red-and-white flannel pajamas. Her hair was mussed, but it was the shadows beneath her eyes that drew his attention. It appeared she hadn't slept any better than him.

"May I come in?" he asked.

She opened the door fully and stepped to the side. He moved past her and into the living room. He noticed that for the first time since they'd decorated the tree that it was darkened. And that was his fault.

Alina took a seat on the couch, crossed her legs and threw a throw blanket over her legs. "Say what you have to say and then go."

Her tone was flat, which was the exact opposite of what he'd been expecting. It wasn't a good sign. If she was angry and yelling at him, he could have defended himself and hopefully gotten through to her. But it was like all of the fight that she'd had in her the whole time he'd known her had gone out of her.

He took a seat in the armchair opposite the couch. He held out the wrap. "Before I forget, here you go." When she didn't make any effort to reach for it, he placed it on the coffee table. "I'm sorry about last night."

Her gaze met his, but it was like a wall had gone up between them because he was no longer able to read her thoughts. "What are you sorry about? That I overheard part of your conversation? Or sorry that I found out you'd already made up your mind to tear down the building?"

His eyes pleaded with her. "I'm sorry about all of it. But you know that our agreement lasts until Christmas Eve, right?"

She shook her head. "It ended last night. I'm not going to let you make a fool of me, especially not with her."

"If you mean your stepmother, I… I was just trying to get her to move right away—to make things easier for you."

Alina's bloodshot gaze met his. "Nothing can make this easy."

"Listen, if you'd hear me out, you'd understand that the building is beyond saving. It failed too many inspections and needs too many repairs."

"What I hear is you making excuses to push through your plan to build your tower here." Alina got to her feet. "I don't think we have anything else to discuss. You need to go. I have your things packed. They're downstairs."

He got to his feet, too. "Alina, don't do this to us."

"Why?"

His mouth opened but wordlessly it closed

again. Silence filled the air as his eyes begged her to forgive him. "Is this really what you want?"

She nodded. "I can't be with someone that isn't honest with me."

"But I didn't lie to you."

"It feels that way. You said you'd wait until Christmas Eve and yet it's days before it. And then to overhear you tell my stepmother, of all people, that your mind is made up about my home, about the home of people that considered you their friend, people that went out of their way to make sure you had the best Christmas party." Her voice cracked with emotion. "Go."

Her words were like rocks being thrown at his heart. He hadn't stopped in that moment with her stepmother to realize the mistake he was making. He'd merely acted rashly to solve a problem—the way he did things in the office—figure out a solution and then act accordingly. Only this wasn't exactly an office problem, it was something much more important.

"I'll make it up to you," he said, "if you'll let me."

"Does that mean I get to keep my home—the homes of my friends?"

He couldn't make that promise because he was already obligated to his board and so many other people. And he had a feeling even if he said she could have the building that things wouldn't go back to the way they used to be between them.

"I'm sorry," he said. He'd never been sorrier in his life.

He moved out the door with a heavy heart. All the while, he felt as though there were still things left unsaid. But when he paused and turned back, the door swung shut with a resounding thud. She obviously didn't feel the same way.

On the elevator ride downstairs, he told himself it was all for the best. He knew that marriage and business didn't mix. He'd witnessed enough arguments between his parents.

They might have remained married but he wasn't sure it was for the best. Neither of them seemed happy. And he didn't want to make Alina as miserable as his mother had been. Alina would be better off without him.

CHAPTER NINETEEN

IT WAS OVER.

It was all over.

And Alina had never been more miserable in her life. She was about to lose her home and she had no idea where to move. And with this being Christmas week, there were no real estate agents to help her.

Graham said his company had already contacted some people and would be forwarding information about available units by the new year. But she didn't want to wait that long. If she had to move, she just wanted to get it over with—the sooner, the better.

She was never one to just sit around and wait for things to happen, she liked to take the lead, but for the moment, she had to work. Even though some people were able to take off for the holiday, she was previously scheduled to work up to and including Christmas Eve.

It was the day before Christmas Eve that Alina stopped by Merryweather's apartment. She'd realized that she'd forgotten to give him the shawl that went with the beautiful gown she'd worn to the Snow Ball.

"I'm really sorry for not returning this sooner," she said as she handed it over. "I… I don't have a good excuse. I forgot." The truth was she'd been so upset with Graham and the fact she'd let herself fall for him that she hadn't thought of much else.

"It's all right, my dear." Merryweather studied her. "You haven't been sleeping well, have you?"

Was it that obvious? She'd have to start using more makeup to hide the shadows beneath her eyes. She didn't want anyone else questioning the reason behind her restless nights.

"I'm okay." *Liar. Liar.*

"I've noticed that Graham hasn't been around since the party."

She swallowed hard. This was why she'd been avoiding people, but she'd have to explain to them sooner or later. "Our arrangement is over." The breath hitched in her throat as she prepared to tell her friend the worst of it. "And…and Graham has decided to go ahead with the demolition of this building."

For a moment Merryweather didn't say a word. His face didn't give away his thoughts, but she knew he had to be as devastated as she felt. After all, this was his home, too. She wasn't quite sure how long he'd lived here, but he'd been here her entire life and then some.

"I'm sorry." She felt like she'd let down everyone in the building—the people she cared about, the people she thought of as family.

"Are you sure about this? He seemed like he really liked it around here."

"I'm sure. I overheard him talking to my stepmother at the ball."

Merryweather's bushy white brows rose. "I'm surprised he'd bother with her."

"I am, too."

"And that's when you heard he was going ahead with his plans to put the new tower here?" Merryweather didn't seem to want to believe what she was telling him and she couldn't blame him. It was a lot to take in.

"Yes." Her gaze lowered to her laced fingers. "I just thought…" She shook her head. "Never mind."

"You thought what? That he'd changed his mind? You thought you'd opened his eyes to just how special this place was with such friendly and caring people?"

She lifted her gaze to meet his. "That's it exactly. And then to find out that he confided his plans to my stepmother, of all people."

"You thought he should have talked to you first?"

She nodded. "Don't you think so? I mean, we did have an agreement."

"But did he promise you that he would speak to you first?"

"No. I just assumed that since it was our deal, I'd be the first to know."

"And did he say why he told her first? Was it possible he'd uttered the words in the heat of the moment?"

She thought back over the tumultuous confrontation at her apartment. She'd been so hurt—so devastated—that she hadn't given him much time to explain himself.

Her stepmother knew exactly how to press people's buttons. Was that the reason Graham had said something to her? Had he found out that her stepmother and stepsisters connived to make her miss the ball? Would he have cared enough to come to her defense?

The possibilities raced through her mind. Had she not given Graham enough credit? Had she just jumped to the conclusion that he would let her down like the other people in her life had done? Had she judged Graham too quickly?

She gave herself a mental shake, trying to clear her head. "I don't know what to think."

"You won't know until you ask. But I did happen by Dorian's place this morning on my way to Joe's apartment to drop off a book he'd asked to read and imagine my surprise when I saw her door open and the apartment empty of furniture. No nothing."

"They've moved out already? Even with the bonus for an early move out, we don't have to be out of here until after the beginning of the year."

"I don't know but something sure got them moving fast." There was a twinkle in his eyes as though he knew something he just wasn't saying. "You might want to give Graham another chance. There might be more going on here than either of us knows." His gaze moved to the plate of sugar cookies she'd placed on the end table. "Would those happen to be for me?"

She glanced over at the plate. She'd totally forgotten that she'd brought them for him. "Yes, they are. But they won't be as good as the ones Graham brought you."

"Don't be so sure. Things baked with love always taste the best."

Tears stung her eyes. She blinked repeatedly. "You always know just what to say."

"Now stop wasting time here. Go find Graham and this time listen with your heart."

She pondered his words as she walked to the door. She honestly didn't know what she was going to do where Graham was concerned. She hesitated to go see him, as much as her heart urged her to do so. She still didn't know if she could love a man who destroyed her home and took away her family.

She hadn't said anything to Merryweather because she hadn't wanted to upset him, but she was convinced that this would be their last Christmas together.

Nothing had gone according to plan.

Not one single thing. And Graham had no one to blame but himself.

Before Alina had entered his life, he was driven by one thing—success. He'd told himself the most important thing was proving himself to the board, but deep inside he knew he had to prove to himself that he was capable of stepping into his father's shoes.

He'd been in awe of the man growing up. After all, his father was regularly in the paper for making one successful deal after the next. And he'd been named Man of the Year by one of the most renowned financial publications. His father was certainly well-recognized and well-respected in the business world. To live up to his memory was a daunting task.

And then to learn that his father's successful career was in part a charade. In later years, the company had been in trouble, had been playing a shell game, trying to hide its deficiencies.

There was nothing harder than stepping into

a new job and finding nothing was as it seemed. And just when he'd been about to turn it all around, Alina stepped into his life. She was all spunk and determination. And she was the roadblock to his success. But at the time, he hadn't realized she was exactly what he needed to open his eyes to the fact that there was more to life than business and success. A happy life isn't about the big things that happen now and again, but rather it's about the little things you do on a daily basis that bring a smile to someone's face.

She'd also showed him how much family meant. Alina clung to her apartment because it was the last tangible link she had to her parents. And she was willing to do whatever it took to hang on to it.

And yet here he was standing on his pride, unwilling to admit that his mother might have made some good points about making room in his life for both business and family. She'd been so sure he'd end up like his father and he'd gone right ahead and proved her right.

But it wasn't too late to change. If he wanted to be the man Alina deserved, he needed to do more than talk the talk, he needed to walk the walk.

He grabbed his phone. Before he could talk himself out of it, he dialed an old but familiar number.

The phone rang once. Twice.

"Graham, is that you?"

"Yes, Mom. It's me."

It wasn't until then that he realized how much he missed hearing his mother voice. And he was surprised to find that she didn't sound mad at him. She didn't bring up their last argument or throw his words back in his face. She was just genuinely happy to speak to him.

He couldn't believe he'd put this conversation off for so long. "Mom, I'm sorry it's been so long since we talked."

"I'm sorry, too. I should have tried harder to understand how important the business is to you."

"Are you saying that you now understand?"

There was a pause. "I didn't want to, not at first. Your father always told me when he retired he'd make more time for us—that we'd travel the world. And then we lost him—and his promises died with him. I was so angry that I blamed the business. And because I loved you, I didn't want to lose you to the business, either. But I pushed so hard that it's exactly what I did."

"I should have been more understanding. I'm sorry. I was so caught up in proving to myself that I was good enough to fill Dad's shoes that I didn't realize what you were going through."

"And now?"

"Now, I have the biggest dilemma of my life."

And so he told her about Toliver Tower—tying the past to the future. It was meant to be Graham's mark upon the company, pulling him out from behind his father's shadow. And then he mentioned how it was destroying his relationship with the woman he loved.

Yes, he loved Alina. The problem was he'd figured that important bit out a little too late.

"If you love this woman as much as you say you do, you'll find a way to work things out," his mother said.

It wasn't the solution he'd been hoping for. In fact, it wasn't a solution at all. It left him in the same position he'd been in at the start of this conversation.

"I've been trying to find a compromise to make everyone happy, but I don't think there is one." He'd barely slept for days, trying to find a way to fix things with Alina. "No matter what I decide, people are going to be disappointed and angry."

"Then it sounds to me like you might as well follow your heart."

Or follow Alina's heart. If she were to know all of the details of the Stirling's physical condition and the projected plans for the new building, would she make the same decision?

He wasn't sure, but a plan was starting to form. "Thank you, Mother. You've been a huge help."

"Can we get together over the holidays?" she asked with a hopeful tone in her voice.

"I'd like that." He thought of Alina and hoped she'd be a part of it, too.

"Graham?"

"Yes."

"Thank you for calling. It means the world."

"I'm just sorry it took this long."

And he meant it. He'd let his pride get in the way of their relationship. It wouldn't happen again.

Now, he had a very serious decision to make. Because through it all, he'd learned that he was a better man with Alina in his life. She made him see the bright side of life even on the darkest day and she made him laugh, even at himself. He needed her. He just hoped she needed him, too.

So his big decision really wasn't such a big decision, after all. It didn't matter how many times he considered the proposal, he'd choose Alina every time.

And it wasn't just Alina that he'd grown fond of. It was also the people of the Stirling—well, most of them. Thankfully he'd given Alina's stepmother and stepsisters a strong enough incentive to move out. Hopefully they'd moved far away.

So how did he make Alina and the Stirling residents happy? By keeping their building standing. But even if he wanted to do that, there were problems. The whole building needed to be re-plumbed, rewired, new windows...the list went on. It would cost more to fix than to rebuild.

But the more he thought about it, the more he felt certain his plan would work. He rushed to grab his coat on his way to the door. He didn't care how late it was. He started dialing his employees. He had a plan and he needed their help. This couldn't wait.

CHAPTER TWENTY

SHE'D MISSED HIM.

Alina didn't know that it was possible to miss someone so much, but she felt the loss from her life clear down to the depths of her bones.

Amid her misery, Christmas Eve arrived in a flurry of activity. Everyone was making plans to move out. Moving boxes had been piled in the hallways, waiting to be filled so that Graham's people could move them to either storage or their new apartment.

Alina hadn't packed one solitary item. Just the thought of it turned her stomach. Instead she'd taken every single shift available at the café. She'd had to stay busy. It'd been the only way to get through the pain of losing Graham. And that was why she'd agreed to take over someone else's shift on Christmas Eve.

The café was about to close early when the front door opened. Alina turned to tell whoever it was that they were closed, and her gaze met Graham's. Her words hovered at the back of her mouth and then dissipated. What was he doing here?

Alina stared deeply into Graham's eyes, drinking in his very essence. But was it possible to move past everything that had happened? Could she truly love a man who took away her home—the place where her most precious memories lived?

Her heart pounded out its hope. It wanted Graham back at all costs. But her mind said to move cautiously because he'd hurt her once and she didn't know how she'd live through another heartbreak.

She continued to stare at him as he approached her. She dug deep and found her courage. She swallowed hard. She hoped when she spoke that her voice didn't give away her nervousness.

"Why are you here?" she asked as they stood in the middle of the Christmas Café. She hadn't seen him since he'd returned her shawl.

"I had to come. There's something important you need to see."

Her eyes widened. "Has something happened? Is it the building?"

"Calm down, Alina." Graham went to reach out to her—to comfort her—but then he hesitated and lowered his arm back to his side. "It's nothing like that."

Relief rushed through her body. "Then whatever it is, you don't need me." She just wanted him to go away. Seeing him—being so close to him and yet they'd never been so far apart—was killing her on the inside.

"But you don't understand, you're the key to everything. Please come with me."

"I… I can't." She glanced around to find her coworkers staring at them. "I have to close up."

Sally stepped forward. "It's okay. We can manage. Why don't you go find out what he wants?"

Alina turned to her friend and glared. She was supposed to be helping Alina out of this extremely awkward position with her ex—wait, was Graham her ex? They'd never really talked through the specifics of their relationship.

"Please, Alina. I think you're going to like this." Graham's eyes pleaded with her.

"I don't know."

Just then her coworkers started with a low chant of "Go. Go. Go." It grew in volume. Alina's mouth gaped. These people were pushing her to do something her mind said was a mistake even as her heart longed to find out what he wanted. What was so urgent?

Sally handed over her coat and purse. Alina's mouth opened to protest but Sally gave her a gentle push toward the door.

"Have fun," Sally said. "And merry Christmas." Alina begrudgingly walked to the door. When she paused and glanced back, everyone was still staring at them. The chanting had stopped and instead they all wore pleased grins. They were traitors. Each and every one of them.

She shrugged on her coat and then walked through the door Graham held open for her. Once they were on the sidewalk, she noticed a black sedan with the driver opening the door for them.

"Where…" Her voice wavered. She swallowed hard, willing her nerves to calm. "Where are we going?"

"Back to the past."

"The past?" She was confused. He was talking in riddles.

"And the future."

He was absolutely no help. What was he trying to tell her? And why was he being so cryptic about it all?

"Please, Alina. I promise it'll be worth it."

She got in the car. They slowly made their way through the congested streets. She felt as though she should make conversation to break the awkward silence. But then, just as quickly, she realized that none of this was her idea. If he didn't like the quiet he could do something about it. But for the moment, he seemed inclined to ride along in silence.

Frustrated, she turned away from him to stare out the window. With each passing block, the scenery became more familiar. If they made a right up here, she was certain where they were going.

And then they turned right. They were headed home—back to the Stirling. Did this mean he'd changed his mind about tearing it down? As excitement lifted her heart, reality brought her back down to earth. If he'd changed his mind, he would have told her by now.

So if this meeting wasn't about the apartment building, was it about them getting back together? The thought tempted and teased her.

But to give in to her desires—to even consider getting back together—she needed more than he'd been willing to give her before. She needed a commitment that she—that their relationship—would come before business. She had to know he loved her. Anything less wasn't enough. Anything less wouldn't be fair to either of them.

And Graham had already told her he couldn't make the commitment a marriage needed to survive. So this was all just a painful waste of time.

She turned to Graham. "I don't think this is a good idea."

He stared deep into her eyes. "Do you trust me?"

This was such an important question. Without trust they didn't have any chance of a future. She didn't have to debate the answer to this question because it was something she knew instinctively.

She nodded.

He smiled and reached out to take her hand in his. And that's how they were sitting when the car pulled to a stop in front of the Stirling.

"Come on." Graham opened the door before the driver could do it. He stepped out and then turned back to offer her his hand.

She stepped outside the car as a light snow started to fall. "Graham, I don't understand. What can you say to me here that you couldn't say back at the restaurant?"

"It's not what I can say, it's what I can show you." His eyes pleaded with her not to fight him. "Just give me five minutes. If you don't like what you see, I'll go away and you'll never have to see me again."

Five minutes. In some instances, that was no time at all. But with her heart hanging on his every word, it was agonizingly long. And yet, she was dying to know what had him going out of his way. After all, if this was about the sale, he had everything he wanted. Every resident had agreed to move early.

"Okay." Her heart raced. She didn't know what he had planned but she hoped it was something good.

CHAPTER TWENTY-ONE

WHAT WAS HE up to?

As they quietly made their way to her apartment. Alina's stomach shivered with nerves. Graham was acting so strange and she had no idea what to make of it.

Once she stepped inside, she was surprised to find the Christmas tree lit up. Prince was stretched out beneath the tree, quietly observing them. Alina knew she hadn't turned the lights on. The tree had been dark since the night of the ball. She stepped toward the tree to turn them off and saw two large Christmas presents sitting on the coffee table with a smaller package sitting in the middle.

She turned to Graham. "Did you do this?"

He nodded. His serious expression didn't give anything away. It wasn't like they'd parted friends, so why would he buy her Christmas presents?

Once their coats were off and they were seated

in the living room, she turned to him. "You shouldn't be buying me gifts."

He stared at her with regret in his eyes. "I'm sorry it took me so long to figure things out."

What was he saying? Was he saying he wanted them to get back together? She tried to subdue her excitement when she reminded herself that it was going to take more than a present to fix things. Still, she wondered what he'd picked out for her.

He handed her the smallest of the packages. She stared down at the red-foil-wrapped box with a satin bow. It was very light, as though there was nothing in it. What was it?

The paper was so pretty that she wanted to unwrap it carefully to save it but her fingers were clumsy with nerves and her need to see what was inside had her ripping it off to find a plain white rectangular box. Her questioning gaze lifted to meet Graham's.

"Go ahead. I promise it won't bite."

It was all the encouragement she needed. She lifted the lid and then pulled back the red tissue paper, finding a large gold key ornament. She lifted it by its thin red satin ribbon.

She held it in front of her. It was pretty enough. She turned her attention back to Graham. "I don't understand."

"You will."

He moved to the other side of the coffee table. He knelt down. "That key goes with one of these." He reached out to the first package and lifted the box.

What was beneath the fancy wrapping was a model of a building. She could only surmise that it was a replica of Toliver Tower. She wanted to hate it, she really did. But it was a pretty building. It had modern lines but historical characteristics. It wasn't the cold, nondescript building that she'd imagined. Someone had taken their time in designing it.

Then without a word, Graham lifted the lid on the other package to reveal a model of the Stirling—the place she'd called home all of her life. She marveled at the exactness of the miniature, right down to the bushes next to the front door.

Her gaze lifted. "They are amazing."

He nodded and then came to sit beside her. "The man who makes them is a real artist. But I didn't bring them here for you to merely admire. Back when you made me that deal, I was so sure I knew what I wanted in life. I knew I didn't want to repeat my parents' mistakes. And truth be told, I didn't repeat theirs. I made all of my own mistakes. I thought for so long that I could have only one thing or the other, but I never thought I could have both."

Her heart started to beat faster. She told herself not to get too excited because she didn't want to get her heart broken. But she knew it was too late for that. She was totally invested in this—in them. But she needed him to spell it out to her in detail.

"Graham, I don't know what you're trying to tell me. Have both what?"

"The business, it's all I've thought of since I was a kid. I needed to prove myself to my father, but most of all, I needed to prove to myself that I was good enough to be CEO. And I did, but I found out that being a success in the business world wasn't as fulfilling as I'd thought it would be. I need someone to share it with."

"But you did it. You pushed through the sale of the Stirling in record time, and your building—" she glanced at the coffee table where the replicas sat "—will be completed ahead of schedule. It's everything you wanted. Your name will be on the building and your board has to be duly impressed."

"But they aren't who I want to impress. That's what I'm trying to tell you in my fumbled way. It means nothing without you. I love you, Alina."

Had she really heard him correctly? "You… you do?"

He nodded. "I fell for you that first day in the café."

"You did?"

He smiled at her as he took her hand in his, his thumb gently stroking her skin. "Why else would I take you up on that arrangement to take over the handyman duties when I didn't have a clue what I was doing?"

"You didn't seem terribly lost."

"That's because I had YouTube videos to guide me and real handymen on speed dial when I got myself in a jam."

"But you never complained."

"And take a chance of you firing me? No way. I was having too much fun getting to know you. The better I got to know you and the residents of the Stirling, the more everything started to change."

"You mean you finally figured out what's so special about this place?"

He nodded. "I did. Now I have a question for you. In which of these two—" he gestured to the buildings "—would you like to spend your future?"

She looked at him. Then she turned to the building models. And then she gazed back to him. "I thought you'd already made up your mind. The Stirling needs too many repairs."

"And if you want to remain here, I'll see that the repairs are done. It may not be pretty for a while and I can assure you it will be noisy, but I will make it happen."

Her gaze searched his. She had to be imagining all of this. He couldn't be serious. "But all of your plans…"

"Plans are made to be changed."

With each word he spoke, she was falling further in love with him. "But this is your chance to make your mark on the company."

"And you've taught me there's more to life than business. Something my mother tried to tell me years ago, but I was too stubborn to hear."

Hope bloomed in her chest. "Does this mean you spoke to your mother?"

"I did. We had a long conversation and we're getting together for the holidays. She's eager to meet you."

"I'm so happy for both of you."

He stood and then held out his hand to help her to her feet. When they were both standing close, he stared into her eyes. "Alina, you've shown me what's important in life. And it's not business or making a name for myself, it's so much more than all of that. It's having people in your life that want to spend time with you—people that are there for you through the good and bad. And most of all, it's people like you that give me time to figure out that I'm wrong."

"What were you wrong about?"

"Love. I thought that having a successful career meant having to choose it over love. But you showed me that it's not an either/or proposition."

She smiled. "I did all of that?"

"You did. I love you, Alina. And I can't imagine my life without you in it."

"I love you, too."

He pulled her close and claimed her lips with his own. Her heart soared. This was the best Christmas ever. Her feet felt as though they were floating.

He pulled back, ending the kiss much too soon. "I have one more present for you."

He moved to his jacket and withdrew a wrapped box from the pocket. The breath caught in Alina's lungs. Could it be?

She told herself that she was getting too carried away. But she couldn't stop herself from hoping they would be together forever. Even then, it wouldn't be long enough.

He turned back to her and held out the gift with the tiniest gold bow. "This is for you."

It wasn't until she accepted the box that she noticed the tremor in her hands. Her mind raced for all of the things that could fit in the little box. Each time she thought of a diamond ring, she pushed aside the thought. It had to be something else. Maybe a bracelet to match her snowball necklace.

With her hands not quite cooperating, she obliterated the wrapping paper. Inside she found a little aqua box. As she read the name of the famous jeweler printed on the lid, she gasped.

She lifted the lid and found yet another box. But this box was made of black velvet. Tears of joy rushed to her eyes. She blinked them away. For a moment, she just stood there staring at the little box that fit in her palm.

Graham reached for the box. "Perhaps I should take it."

Her gaze met his. She had so many questions but her mouth totally refused to work. Of all the times for her to be speechless.

Graham opened the box. The overhead light caught the brilliant diamond and made it sparkle. Her heart was beating like crazy. Was this really happening?

And just to prove it, Graham got down on one knee. "Alina, I didn't know it for so long but you are what I've been searching for. You are the morning sunshine that lights my days. You are the comfort I seek after a long day. And you are the best friend that I've ever had. I love you with all of my heart. Will you marry me?"

Tears of joy splashed onto her cheeks as she nodded her head because she was afraid her voice would fail her once more, but she tried to speak, anyway. "Yes. Yes, I will."

He drew her back into his arms and this time when he kissed her, it was so full of love. She'd never been happier in her life.

And she knew that no matter where she went in the world that her home would always be with Graham. It wasn't a building. It was the memories. And they would make plenty. And it wasn't the hallways or the rooms. It was the love in her heart that had room enough for everyone she cared about...most especially her real-life Prince Charming.

EPILOGUE

Two years later... Toliver Tower

HOME AT LAST.

Alina Toliver placed the last table setting on the long row of tables that stretched from her living room into the dining room. Graham had had his people deliver the tables and chairs from his office the day before and now it was all set for this evening's Christmas Eve dinner.

Prince took a bit to adjust to his new surroundings, but now he thought he was in charge. He rubbed over Alina's ankles as she straightened each place setting. She smiled at how everything was at last falling into place. She hoped everything would go perfectly this evening. After all, this was their first Christmas in their new home.

In the past couple of years, the Stirling residents had been split apart as there was no one place available in the city to accommodate so many dislocated residents. She had dearly missed her friends, but Graham had kept her distracted planning their wedding. She glanced down at her sparkling diamond engagement ring. One month ago to the day, she'd received the matching diamond wedding band. It wasn't the ring's beauty that meant so much to her, it was the promise it carried—Graham would love her forever. And she him.

"Still admiring them, I see." Graham's voice interrupted her thoughts.

She lowered her hand to her side. "I was just thinking that today's our one-month anniversary."

"That long already?" He stepped up close to her, placing his hands on her waist. "It's only the first of many anniversaries."

"Do you know how nice that sounds?"

He leaned down, placing his lips on hers. She immediately leaned into his embrace. It didn't matter how many times he kissed her, it still felt like the first. Her heart pitter-pattered as desire pumped through her veins.

"Hey, you two newlyweds, aren't we supposed to be getting ready for a party?"

Alina immediately jumped but Graham refused to let her go. He wrapped his arm around her waist, pulling her to his side. Prince scampered over to hide behind them.

"Hello, Mother," Graham said. "We didn't hear you arrive."

"Obviously." His mother smiled. "You two look good together. Any news about grandchildren?"

"Mother." Graham frowned at her. "Stop pushing."

"Who's pushing? With the way you two look at each other, it's a safe bet."

Alina smiled. She enjoyed seeing Graham reconnecting with his mother. It was long overdue. She moved out of her husband's hold and went to greet her mother-in-law. Sharon Toliver was tall and slender, her dark hair the same shade as her son's. When Sharon smiled, it lit up her brown eyes. Alina realized that Graham may have inherited his father's business acumen but he'd also inherited his mother's warmth.

Alina reached out and hugged Sharon. "Welcome."

As Alina took Sharon's coat, his mother looked around. "This place is beautiful. Not like that stone-and-granite mausoleum that Graham stayed in at the office building. This place has warmth. It looks like a home, not a showpiece. Alina, you have done a marvelous job."

"Thank you. But we—" she motioned to Graham, who was now standing beside her "—did it together."

"You are good for my son."

"And he's good for me," Alina quickly added, meaning it wholeheartedly.

Sharon's gaze moved to the collection of tables. "My, you're expecting a lot of guests. People from the office?"

"Just family," Alina said.

Ding-dong.

Prince dashed back to the bedroom. Alina smiled and shook her head. He might be bossy with her and Graham, but when it came to strangers, he made like a ghost and disappeared.

"And there are our guests now." Alina moved to the door, anxious to see her family all together again.

And this would be just the first of many such occasions because Graham had invited all willing Stirling residents to move into the top two floors of the newly finished Toliver Tower. They were a family once more.

Alina swung the double doors wide open and there stood her family in their Christmas sweaters, Santa hats and smiles. In the front stood Merryweather, carrying a bottle of wine with a red bow on it as he held the leash to his sweet rescue dog, Bentley. Her heart swelled with love for both of them.

"You all came," she said.

"Of course we did," Merryweather said. "Where else would we be on Christmas Eve but with family?"

Alina turned back to her mother-in-law. "Sharon, do you remember my family from the wedding?"

"Yes, I do." Sharon smiled as she moved to Alina's side to greet everyone.

After everyone arrived, Alina stepped back, taking in the happy scene. For a moment, she watched as the people interacted. It was then she admitted that she'd been wrong. Having a new building hadn't changed anything. They were still the people she loved. And she was blessed enough to be loved back.

Just then Graham moved up beside her and slipped his arm around her waist. "Something on your mind?"

"How did I get to be so lucky? Our family isn't bound by bloodlines. It's made up of the people of our hearts."

He turned to her. He pointed up. She lifted her head, finding that they were standing under the mistletoe. A smile pulled at her lips. She lifted up on her tiptoes. "I love you."

"I love you, too."

And then she leaned into his arms and they kissed. It didn't last long but it was filled with love and a promise of more to come. But first they had a potluck dinner to enjoy followed by their Secret Santa gift exchange. Everything was as it should be that Christmas. Everyone was home.

* * * * *

*If you enjoyed this story,
check out these other great reads from
Jennifer Faye*

The Italian's Unexpected Heir
The CEO, the Puppy and Me
The Prince and the Wedding Planner
Her Christmas Pregnancy Surprise

All available now!